Meant to be Chased

By Jessica Frederick

This book is dedicated to several people. First off, my cousin Monte Tudor-Long for helping me find my voice, and insisting that he wanted to read this book even though I assured him he wasn't my target demographic.

Secondly, my parents for instilling my love to read at a very young age.

Third, to my friends who have stuck by me throughout this process and understood that I was going to be super lame every November for the last three years until this project was complete.

Last, but certainly not least, this second printing is dedicated to Mindy's mom for her willingness to take the time to proofread my poorly typed first draft.

The life and times of Violet Montgomery.

I went through high school sitting in a glass case whilst all the girls stared at me like I was an alien and the guys avoided me as if I had some sort of disease in my lady parts. To say I was socially awkward would be an understatement.

Okay, listen. Like any good story, there's a bit of background. And I'm not good at laying it out. So bear with me. I promise that it will get better; you just have to sift through some boring crap to get to the good stuff. Can you live with that?

I was seventeen years old before anything particularly good happened. Fortunately for me, until this happened I had one best friend, Willow Phan. My family was also somewhat supportive, however we didn't always see eye to eye. My parents were relatively young when I was born and we struggled a lot in my early childhood. Once my dad finished dentistry school and got a job at a dental practice we were able to make ends meet. When I was ten years old my parents decided that we could now afford to have more kids. That's when my sister Liana was born. Two years later came my brother Daniel.

After my brother and sister were born, my parents spent most of their time taking care of them. By this point I was twelve years old and apparently old enough to take care of myself. Luckily, my mom's sister, Trudi, was there for me. She helped a lot after my parents' nuclear family was achieved and I was left out.

I was kind of the black sheep of my family. I didn't look like my parents or siblings. I had dark brown hair and green eyes, while the rest of them had blond hair and blue eyes. I've always been short for my age, whereas my parents are both rather tall. In fact, by the time my little sister was seven, she was almost as tall as me. In all reality, I didn't fit in with my family at all, physically or ideologically.

I went to Lincoln High School, which sounds nice but was really a big utilitarian brick building that I'm sure was often mistaken for a factory. It was bleak looking, which didn't make anyone want to be there. Not that anyone really wanted to be in high school anyway. Especially me; I definitely wanted to spend as little time with these idiots as possible. I had this thing I liked to call "people hate." It got me in trouble a lot.

At the beginning of April, my junior year in high school, another typical school day full of obnoxious people and droning teachers had just ended. Willow and I walked through the parking lot to our cars, which were typically parked next to each other.

"I'll see you tomorrow," Willow said, over the roof of her car.

"See ya," I called back. As Willow ducked into her car, I made awkward eye contact with the infamous Carter Greenspan who had been standing behind her. I rolled my eyes and got into my car.

Carter and I had been best friends our whole lives. In fact, our mothers had been friends since college. They had introduced our fathers to each other and gone on double dates. They were married within a few months of each other and members of each other's wedding parties. Carter and I were born within less than a month of each other. It was almost as if it had been planned. After that, it was all Sunday barbecues and family outings. For our entire lives Carter and I had spent every day after school as well as most weekends together until we were in seventh grade.

That was when Anna Ryan started a rumor that I liked Carter. After that he seemed to want nothing to do with me and started hanging out with her instead. Somehow, the rumor made him believe that I was obsessed with him, although for the past thirteen years I had never shown obsessive tendencies. For some bizarre reason he could hang out with a group of 'popular' girls who worshipped the ground he walked on much easier than he could hang out with the one girl he'd been friends with all his life.

A few weeks after Carter and I had stopped hanging out, Willow moved to town. We became fast friends and have been ever since. As middle school went on I slowly got over the fact that Carter didn't want to be friends with me. By the time we entered high school nothing about the situation really bothered me. In fact, I actually found Carter Greenspan slightly ridiculous.

Carter and Anna had been in an official relationship for a few months now, after a disturbing amount of back and forth. It made complete sense, though. Carter was the star of the baseball team, and Anna was the typical Polly Pocket cutout 'popular' girl. All of Carter's friends were dating one of Anna's friends, with the exception of his best friend, Liam, who had it bad for Willow; a fact to which she pretended to be oblivious.

This is why I found the next four seconds of my life annoying, yet confusing. As Carter walked to his car, Anna on his arm, his eyes met mine briefly. He smiled, and waved at me. I slammed my door shut in response and started my engine, choosing to ignore him rather than acknowledge him. This was fair, considering that was how he had treated me for the past four years.

I drove home the same way I do every day which takes me right past Carter's house, two houses down from mine. I parked on the street and went inside. No one was home yet. My parents were at work and my siblings were at an after school program that I would have to pick them up from at five.

I walked up the stairs, glancing at my reflection in the long mirror in the hallway. My long brown hair was messy, but that was normal. The black eyeliner I was wearing was smudged. I wiped some of the eyeliner off with my finger, and stepped into my bedroom.

I opened up my laptop and logged into Facebook, because I wasn't really concerned with starting my homework before I had to go pick up my brother and sister from school. After disregarding a few unimportant notifications and Farmville requests and scrolling through mindless status updates, I noticed Willow was online, so I sent her a message.

"Hey, what's going on?" I asked.

"Just digging into my calculus. You? " was her response.

"Planning a wedding," I informed her.

"Whose?" she asked.

"Mine and Carter's. Just call me Mrs. Greenspan."

"Is that so?"

"Well, he finally acknowledged my existence. I can die happy now," I told her.

At this point in our friendship, Willow had obviously heard about all the Carter drama of our middle school days. When we were in eighth grade my favorite defense mechanism was to joke as if I were actually obsessed with Carter. This habit (mostly) ceased when I realized I didn't care anymore.

"Well bless your little heart. Did you faint? Are you alright? Do you need me to bring you a casserole and tend to your every need while you're in this state of perpetual bliss?"

"Interaction was limited," I told her. "He had a Barbie dangling from his arm. "

"Tough break, kid," Willow said.

"Well there's always tomorrow. Maybe this time he'll actually talk to me."

"And if you don't die from shock, maybe you can be friends again."

I laughed out loud and typed quickly. "Do you think you'll be able to replace me on such short notice?"

"I'm sure I'll manage," she said.

"You can start hanging out with Liam," I told her.

"Bite me," she retorted.

"Maybe tomorrow. I have to go pick up the kiddos," I sent before shutting my laptop and leaving.

The rest of my afternoon was nothing spectacular. I picked the kids up from school, went home and had dinner with my family. My parents talked about their jobs and what had happened that day. They asked the kids about their riveting elementary school lives. They paid little to no attention to me. Average night.

After dinner I did my homework and went to bed like any other seventeen-year-old girl who only had one friend would do.

That night, I had a rather disturbing dream. I was swinging on a wooden swing built between two ivy-covered trees in one of the most beautiful backyards I had ever seen. In one corner, there was a small pond, with a stream that flowed into a larger pond. Next to the ponds was a cute Victorian-style bench and the whole area was surrounded with white and purple flowers. I immediately recognized this as the Greenspan's backyard from the countless times I had played there as a child.

As I pumped my legs to make the swing go higher I saw my white mary-janes, complete with ruffled socks, and the hem of the dress that I typically wore to church when I was nine years old, which hit my legs just above my awkwardly knobby knees. I looked to my left and saw the sandy haired nine-year-old version of Carter who was also dressed as if he had just come from church.

"Vi!" Carter called, motioning for me to follow him.

I stopped kicking but wouldn't drag my feet on the ground because I didn't want to get my favorite shoes dirty. "I'll be there in a minute!" I called back waiting for the swing to slow down. Once it was slow enough to safely jump off, I did, landing on my feet and running toward Carter laughing.

Carter led me to a willow tree in the other corner of the yard and sat down at the base of it. He patted the ground next to him, indicating that I should sit there, which I did hesitantly because I didn't want to get my dress dirty.

Carter nervously pulled grass out of the ground and tore it up, leaving it in a little pile in front of him. "You know what, Vi?" he said after a minute.

"What?" I asked. Even nine-year-old me was annoyed when people couldn't get right to the point.

"I love you," Carter told me.

I laughed, thinking it must have been a joke. Carter was my best friend. We had known each other for forever. He wasn't allowed to love me. But before I could respond, he leaned forward and quickly kissed me on the lips. As soon as it was over he got up

7

and ran away. I got up as fast as I could and chased him around the yard.

I woke up with a start. The dream had upset me, mostly because it wasn't really a dream at all, but more of a memory. After that had happened, he had pretended it hadn't. Whether he had forgotten about it or not, in the next four years it had never been brought up. I never mentioned it because I didn't want to embarrass him, and since he hadn't tried kissing me since, I assumed he hadn't wanted to. I also reminded myself frequently that we were nine years old and neither of us knew what any of it meant.

Monotony at its finest.

I woke up the next morning and got ready for school as usual. The only difference between this morning and any other morning were the flashbacks to my subconscious memory of the first kiss that I had nearly forgotten about.

School was repetitive as usual; the same obnoxious people and the same droning teachers. The day went by slowly with little eventfulness but finally, at three-fifteen, it was over and I could go to my Aunt Trudi's house, which was something I often did after school. However, time would be limited this afternoon because I had to be to my part-time job at six.

I parked in the parking lot at Trudi's complex and let myself into her apartment. I made my way to the bedroom where she was standing, in contemplation of which outfit she should wear for her date that night. There was a simple purple dress, a long white skirt with a pink shirt and a green maxi dress.

"I like the purple one," I said, pointing to the dress I was referring to.

"Well then you can borrow it for your next date," Trudi said, picking up the white skirt and pink shirt and walking into the en suite bathroom.

"Don't get your hopes up," I called so she could hear me through the closed door. I sat down on the bed and added "I won't be going on any dates anytime soon."

Trudi pushed the bathroom door open so she could see me while she put in her earrings. "And why not?" she asked, in a disapproving tone.

"No one at school tickles my fancy, I suppose," I said plainly.

"What happened to that one guy?" she asked as she began putting on her makeup.

Trudi had a way of acting like she knew what she was talking about when she really didn't. I had never had a boyfriend serious enough that I would find it necessary to tell my family about it. But Trudi would be the one exception to that rule, so maybe I had mentioned a previous "fling" and forgotten about it. "What guy?" I asked.

"Oh come on Violet, you know who I'm talking about," she said rolling her eyes at me. "Carter Greenspan! You two were inseparable!"

"Yeah, when we were seven!" I retorted, jokingly throwing a pillow at her. "Things change."

"But you're not denying that you would be interested in him," she said raising an eyebrow at me.

"I'm not confirming that I would be interested in him either," I pointed out. "And besides, it would take a lot for me to seriously consider him as an option anyway, you know after he just decided we weren't friends anymore and completely stopped talking to me."

Trudi shrugged her shoulders as if she didn't know what to tell me. Aunt Trudi wasn't very good with the advice aspect of being an adult role model. Whenever she tried giving me advice she would just try relating it to a situation she had been in when she was my age, and let's just say that Aunt Trudi wasn't the best example of proper teenage behavior that there ever was. In most cases I was more relieved when she didn't try to give me advice than I was when she did.

I shrugged back. "He has a girlfriend now anyway," I thought I'd mention before she said anything else.

Trudi gave me a look "Is she cute?" she asked, menacingly.

"Cuter than me," I said under my breath, hoping she wouldn't hear me. Unfortunately she did hear me and cut in before I could give her an actual response.

"Violet Irma, don't let me hear you say anything like that about yourself ever again!" she scolded.

I cringed at the sound of my middle name. Although I was named for the grandmother that practically raised my mom and aunt Trudi, Irma wasn't exactly the name that I would have chosen for myself. I rolled my eyes at her before responding with a simple "It's true though!"

My aunt gave me a dirty look and then turned back toward the mirror to finish preparing for her date. I rolled my eyes again at the back of her head, and flung myself back on the bed. I stayed on the bed watching my aunt prepare for her date until it was time for me to leave for work. I changed into my uniform really fast and then left, after wishing Trudi good luck on her date.

As I drove to work, I replayed the entire conversation with Trudi in my head. She had known about me and Carter not being friends anymore. In fact, she was the first person I told. I rolled my eyes again, knowing that Trudi was trying to get me to go after Carter anyway, because it's what she would have done. Good thing I didn't tell her about him waving to me yesterday. Who knows what she would have made that out to mean.

At this point I was mostly just annoyed. I had gone years without even thinking about Carter Greenspan, and here he was, all up in my life like he had been invited.

I parked in the employee parking lot and made my way upstairs to the food court. I worked at Orange Julius, not because I had an affinity for smoothies and hotdogs, but because they were one of the few places that were willing to hire high school kids under 18 to work minimal hours. I got a few hours a week if they really needed someone to cover a shift. Occasionally Willow and I would work together but she wasn't working tonight.

The first hour of work went by as it always does, as uneventful as the rest of my life. I only had a three hour shift and we were only open for two of those hours. A little after seven-thirty, during a slow period, I was cleaning and organizing the fruit cooler and I looked to the counter to check for customers. I had a customer all right. Carter Greenspan. I furrowed my brow and walked to the counter to take his order.

"What can I get you?" I asked politely.

"I don't know. What do you recommend?" he asked, running a hand through his light brown hair.

I resisted the urge to roll my eyes. "I like the strawberry orange smoothie," I suggested, not hinting to my opinion of his idiocy.

"I'll have that then," he said, smiling at me, showing off his pearly white teeth. He was lucky he got his braces off in sixth grade, or else those popular girls wouldn't have wanted to be friends with him in seventh.

I made his smoothie, and handed it to him. As he paid for it, his hand lingered, touching mine. "Thank you, Violet," he said, still smiling.

"You're welcome," I nodded, choosing not to point out that it was my job and I wasn't giving him any special treatment.

After that, nothing noteworthy happened at work. I closed up shop and went home. After showering and doing homework I went to sleep trying to think about anything but Carter.

At least he doesn't have the clap.

At two-forty-three in the morning, my phone beeped loud enough to wake me up. I groaned as I looked at the alarm clock and saw what time it was. I considered ignoring it, but in the off-chance that it was Trudi, needing a ride, I'd rather get out of bed then let her drive drunk. I picked my phone up from the bed side table and looked at the screen. The text message was from a number that I didn't recognize. I opened the message. All it said was "Come outside".

I rolled out of my bed and moved across my dark bedroom to look out the window that faced the street. Carter was standing on the sidewalk, knowingly looking right at the window I was standing at. I hit reply on my phone and texted back. "Why?"

In less than a minute his response had arrived. "I just want to talk to you."

"At 3 AM?" I texted back, not really happy with the events that were unfolding before my eyes.

"Vi, please," was all his response said.

Grudgingly, I walked down the stairs, looking at myself in the mirror as I passed it. I was wearing striped pajama pants and a blue tank top. My hair was pulled up into a ponytail that had been messy when I put it in, and was now worse from hours of sleeping on it. I shrugged and went outside, being careful not to wake up my parents.

I walked, barefoot, to the spot on the sidewalk where Carter stood waiting. I didn't try to hide my blatant annoyance. I stood in front of him, my arms crossed, and an eyebrow raised, waiting for him to cut to the chase.

"Listen, Vi," he started, which annoyed me even more. He hadn't talked to me aside from a conversation about smoothies at my place of employment in over four years, and here was calling me by the nickname I reserved for my family and friends. It was obvious that I considered him neither at this point. I rolled my eyes as he continued. "I know you're not very happy with me and I wouldn't be either. And that's why I wanted to apologize to you. I know it was years ago, but it shouldn't have happened the way it did... I—"

"But it did happen the way it did," I interrupted. "You can't exactly take the past four years of wasted friendship back and make it all okay!"

"I know I can't, Violet!" he said, beginning to sound angry. "The point is, if I could, I would, okay?"

"Sure, whatever," I said with the wave of a hand. "That's what you pulled me out of bed for? To apologize for something that happened four years ago, even though we haven't talked since?" I didn't even try to hide the anger in my voice.

"I guess," he said with a sigh, once again running his hand through his hair. After a few moments of silence, he sighed again and said "I'm sorry."

I bit my lower lip and stared at him for a moment. "Okay, I forgive you for completely dropping me out of your life when a girl, who happens to be your current *girlfriend,* started a rumor about me which you believed even though we had been friends our entire lives. I'll pretend it never happened."

He stared at me in disbelief for a few seconds. "I'm being serious, Vi. I want to be friends."

"Why is this coming up now anyway?" I asked with a sigh.

Carter stood in silence for a few seconds. "I just miss you," he said finally.

I sighed again. "Okay, friends," I said, mostly just so he would leave and I could go back to bed.

"Can we hang out in the daytime sometime?" he asked.

"Sure. But since it's not daytime, I'm going back to sleep," I said, not even trying to be polite, before turning and going back into the house. I marched back up the stairs and into my bedroom. Before I climbed into my bed, I looked out the window again and saw Carter standing on the sidewalk, looking utterly perplexed.

To be honest, though, I was probably just as perplexed as he was. I don't know what made him decide after four years of non-communication that he wanted to even pretend I existed again, much less be friends. These thoughts ran through my head at every point of contact we'd had in the past three days, and my usual state of confusion about topics like this was getting worse and worse.

I wasn't thrilled at the idea of being friends with Carter, after how he had just completely cut me out of his life, but if he was going to be persistent enough to force me out of bed in the middle of the night, I should probably comply within reason to avoid further sleeping pattern interruptions.

I mean, of course I *wanted* to be friends with him, but I definitely didn't want him to think he could just run back to me and say sorry every time he messed up; especially if it was going to take him four years to realize it.

***

When my alarm went off at seven-fifteen, I could not discern why I was unusually tired. Well, I was a teenager. I was always tired. But for some reason that morning I was more tired than usual.

I sat up in my bed and tried to remember the foggy dream I had had the night before. All I could remember was looking at Carter through my window and then going out to talk to him. Slowly bits of conversation flooded into my brain. Why had I had a dream about Carter apologizing to me? Why was I having dreams about Carter in the first place? This was starting to get out of hand.

I picked up my phone to text Willow and tell her I had had yet another dream about Carter when I saw that I had an unread message from and unsaved number and had another flashback to the dream. This had happened in my dream. I opened the text message. It read "Thanks for getting out of bed for me."

So it wasn't a dream. Carter had really shown up at my house in the middle of the night to apologize to me for the past. And I had really gotten out of bed to let him. Wonderful. I hit reply and typed "Anytime." I hit send before I realized why that could be problematic. "Crap, Violet!" I scolded myself. I saved his number in my phone so that if this sort of thing ever happened again I would be able to ignore him. Next, I texted Willow and told her to meet me at school early because I had a lot to tell her.

I got ready in a hurry which wasn't out of the ordinary, since I typically chose not to care about my appearance. I drove to school and was in my usual spot in the cafeteria by 8:05. Willow arrived shortly after, looking slightly annoyed that I had asked her to be there so early. I didn't care, and I knew she wouldn't after I told her what had happened.

"So you'll never guess who showed up at my house at three AM," I said nonchalantly.

"Hmm…. Carter Greenspan?" she said sarcastically.

"Yeah, actually," I admitted.

Before I could elaborate she said "Yeah right, Violet. Like that would happen."

"Willow, I'm serious!" I said, trying to sound convincing. "Look, read the text messages he sent me." I pushed my phone across the table to her. "I'm telling you, Carter came to my house and stood outside waiting or me so that he could apologize for everything that happened and asked if we could be friends again." As I finished telling her what had happened, I noticed she was looking not at my phone, but behind me. I knew who she was looking at before I even turned around, but decided to look anyway.

There stood Anna, glaring in my direction. It was obvious that she had heard everything I had just said about her boyfriend. Perfect. I looked at Willow, who was now staring at me as if I were a child dying of cancer. How bad could it be really? What was the worst Anna could do? Make my best friend stop talking to me?

I went to my morning classes and by lunch I had heard from several people that Carter and Anna had gotten into a fight over Carter going to some girl's house in the middle of the night. Luckily none of them had heard who the girl was.

By the end of the day it was all anyone was talking about. Lincoln High's golden couple was having trouble in paradise. After my last class for the day I was walking through the cafeteria on my way to the car when I noticed a larger-than-usual crowd in the middle of the cafeteria. As I got closer I heard what sounded like a very heated argument.

"That's not the point, Carter!" Anna shouted at him. "I never said you couldn't choose your own friends. I just don't think I can be okay with my boyfriend meeting up with other girls in the middle of the freaking night!"

"Why is it that big of a deal? It's not like anything immoral happened," Carter defended himself.

"How am I supposed to know that nothing happened, Carter?! You were with *another girl!*" Anna said, obviously deeply hurt by this development. If I didn't already have a passionate dislike for Anna I would almost feel sorry for her. Then I remembered that this was her fault anyway and stopped caring.

"Seriously, Anna," Carter said. "It wasn't another girl. It was just Violet."

I could feel the heat rising to my face. Just Violet? I was livid. I couldn't even process my thoughts. I turned and quietly walked out of the cafeteria, trying not to attract attention. That would only make me look more suspicious. Once I got to the parking lot, I found Willow, who, luckily, had not left yet. I wrenched open the passenger side door and climbed in.

"We're going to Trudi's," I said demandingly, buckling my seatbelt before waiting for her to respond.

Luckily for me, Willow was used to my somewhat erratic behavior. She drove to my aunt's apartment without asking what was wrong because she knew I would unload on both of them when we got there. Instead, she turned the music up really loud, hoping a song on the radio would make my mood better. I didn't bother telling her there wasn't a chance.

We walked into my aunt's house and I threw my stuff on the table in her kitchen. My facial expression must have made it obvious that I was fuming because Trudi stopped what she was doing and just stared at me for a few seconds without saying anything. In normal cases the woman never shut up. I sat down at the table, putting my feet up on my chair and wrapping my arms around my bent legs. Willow sat down at the desktop computer that my aunt had in her kitchen/dining room area and clicked on to Facebook.

"What's wrong, sweetie?" Trudi finally asked me.

After a few seconds without a response, she looked to Willow, who just shrugged. Then I remembered that I hadn't even told Willow what had happened, and now I had some explaining to do. I had to start with the events of the previous night so Trudi would be caught up.

"Last night, well, actually really early this morning, Carter showed up at the house and told me to come outside. When I did he apologized for everything that had happened when we were kids, and asked if we could be friends. I said yes, mostly so he would leave me alone. But this morning when I told Willow about it at school, his girlfriend heard me and got mad at him. Then when I was leaving school they were fighting in the cafeteria... She yelled at him for meeting another girl in the middle of the night and he said I wasn't another girl, I was 'just Violet'."

Trudi and Willow were both staring at me now, but neither of them said anything for a good minute. Trudi finally spoke up.

"Well what did you do?" she asked, as if I were some sort of masochist would was willing to make these situations worse by getting further involved.

"I got in Willow's car and came here," I said simply.

Trudi stared at me as if I were mentally challenged. "Why didn't you say anything?" she asked.

Because I'm already too involved in the situation and didn't even have to try for that," I told her. "I didn't want to be involved with him in the first place and now I'm involved in their relationship. I'm a home wrecker and I don't even like him!"

"Are you going to say something?" she asked hopefully.

"What would I say?" I asked. "All I want to do is hit someone."

"You're allowed to have the initial reaction of wanting to punch him in the face," Trudi told me. "But at some point you're going to have to confront him."

"Whoa, Vi, look at this," Willow said, pointing to something on the computer screen.

I leaned over to get a better look and saw what she was pointing to. Carter's relationship status on Facebook went from "in a relationship" to "Single" about two minutes before.

I snorted. "That will last about thirty seconds."

"When I was in high school," Trudi started. Willow and I both rolled our eyes. We knew where this was going. "There was this guy... Dan. Or was it Dave? Anyway, he was dating... Lois Parks. He dumped her though because she gave him chlamydia, which she got from—"

"Trudi," I interrupted. "I don't think this story is relevant to the situation, so I'm going to let you save it for another time. Anyway, your sister expects me for dinner and Willow will need to take me to my car."

Trudi looked at me as if I had told her that her cat had died; a look which I was sure she had perfected convincing my mother to do stuff for her when she was little. My mother was twelve years older than Trudi.

Willow and I left Trudi's house and drove back to school so I could get my car.

"Do you think he's gonna ask you out?" Willow asked after a prolonged silence.

"What?" I asked, not even able to comprehend what she was saying.

"He's single now. Do you think he's going to ask you out?"

"I'm 'just Violet'," I pointed out. "I'm nothing special."

Willow rolled her eyes at me, turning into the school parking lot. "I'd be willing to bet," she mumbled under her breath.

I opened the passenger door before she had even come to a complete stop. "Thanks. I'll see you tomorrow," I said, slamming the door shut. I got into my car as Willow pulled away, and started the engine, staring off toward the baseball field. I couldn't make out any of the individual players at baseball practice, but I knew Carter was one of them. "Maybe I should just drive my car through the field. Spare no casualty," I said out loud, to just myself.

My phone beeped. I looked at the screen. It was a text from Willow. "Whether he does or doesn't, that doesn't really matter. He's not good enough for you... But you probably shouldn't run over the whole baseball team."

I smiled, glad that I had a best friend that could read my mind. There were times when I was almost thankful that Carter and I had stopped being friends, because who knows if I would have made friends with Willow if I was still friends with him.

I drove home, parked and walked into the house just as my family was getting ready for dinner. I washed my hands and sat down at my usual spot at the table, not necessarily thrilled to be spending time with my family. I was already in a terrible mood, due to the day's events, and didn't want to be around people in general, much less these people.

I poured myself a glass of orange juice and helped my brother and sisters with theirs. My mom brought the last of the food to the table. We said grace (I only joined in to appease them) and we began to eat.

"How was work, honey?" my mother asked my father, which launched him into a story about his enthralling life as a dentist. I tuned it out as best as I could, not interested in stories about him being bitten by children. In my opinion, if you spend four extra years in college to go into a profession where you put your hands in peoples' mouths on a daily basis you're inevitably going to get bit a time or two. That's life.

After my dad finished telling us about his day my mom began to ramble about the PTA meeting she had to go to after dinner, professing her worry that if she was late, Marcy Jo Keller would volunteer her for the elementary school fundraiser which would just be way too time consuming now that she was working down at the library.

I ate quickly. When Daniel and Liana began throwing peas at each other across the table, I took that as my cue to leave. I excused myself, mumbling something about homework, and made my way to my bedroom. Once inside, I shut the door and threw myself down on the bed. What a day! I wanted to curl up on my bed, but then I remembered I had some reading to do for English class. But before I started on that, I was curious about one other thing.

I moved to my desk, intent on getting on the computer, but I spotted my beta fish, Pudge, swimming around his glass bowl. I fed him a few beta fish pellets and continued watching him, imagining how easy it would be to be a fish. All I would have to do is swim around my bowl all day, not worrying about anyone or anything ever. How peaceful the life of a fish must be.

I sighed and flopped down into my desk chair. I opened my laptop and logged into Facebook. As I scrolled down my newsfeed I didn't notice anything interested until I got to what I was looking for.

"Carter Greenspan went from being 'in a relationship' to 'single'." Several random girls from our school had liked it, which was something I never understood. Even if you wanted to get with someone, why would liking that their relationship status had changed to single make them want to be with you? It makes you look bad. Whatever. I scrolled down to read the comments.

Steven Travis said "Dude, she was like a ten tho."

Tyler Jacobs said "Yeah, but she was a bitch. Congrats on getting rid of her."

Liam Powell said "Two words: Bro time!"

But perhaps the two most interesting comments in the entire conversation were between Owen Adams and Cater Greenspan.

Owen said "What are you gonna do about prom, man? You can't go stag!"

Carter's response was "Don't worry. I have a plan. ;)"

I rolled my eyes. I felt legitimately sorry for whatever poor girl he asked, who, of course, wouldn't be smart enough to say no. No one saw through Carter's façade. Girls thought he was the greatest thing ever Parents (especially mine) thought he was the greatest thing ever. He probably even thought he was the greatest thing ever. I was the only one who realized what a jerk he really was. I still didn't understand why he had dragged me out of bed last night to talk to "just Violet." If I was really that unimportant to him, would he really have tried to become friends with me in the middle of the night?

Another thing I found amusing about this conversation was that these guys were so concerned about prom. Sure, junior prom is supposed to be some sort of rite of passage. It's the first year you're allowed to go. It's a tradition that's become almost ritualized among high schoolers. Willow and I had already decided we weren't going, and with only about four weeks left until the event, it would be almost impossible to change our minds now anyway.

As I was about to shut my computer, I heard the noise that indicated an instant message. I looked back at the screen and saw that the message was from Carter. I rolled my eyes yet again and mentally noted that this whole situation was giving my eyes the best work out of their lives.

All the message from Carter said was "Hey! ☺" but that didn't change anything. I wasn't the type of girl who could be mad at someone for something and then just melt at a single word.

"What?" I typed back, implying that he should just say what he wants so I could get on with my life.

"Just wanted to say hi…" was the response Carter gave me. I was beyond annoyed.

"Just wanted to say hi to 'just Violet'? Hmm," I replied, hoping my sarcasm was evident.

"Oh, you heard that?" He asked.

"Who didn't hear it? Everyone in the county heard it."

"Look, Vi. I didn't mean it that way…"

"How DID you mean it then?" I asked.

"I was just trying to get Anna off my back."

"By belittling me and telling her it didn't matter that you showed up to my house in the middle of the night and forced me out of bed because I am *just* Violet? I don't even know why you did that anyway. It's not like you actually want to be friends with me. You had to go to my house in the middle of the night so no one would see you talking to me in the first place."

"Violet, it's not like that and you know it."

"Then tell me what it is like!" I was growing angrier with each response. Just because we hadn't spoken to each other since junior high didn't mean that he didn't know me well enough to know that saying things like that about me in public would upset me.

"I do want to be friends with you. Honestly. I wouldn't have gotten you out of bed if I didn't want to be friends with you. I decided right then that it was so important for us to be friends again that I had to ask you about it immediately. That's why I came to your house in the middle of the night. It had nothing to do with not wanting people to see me. The only reason I called you 'Just Violet' was because I wanted Anna to think that you weren't a threat. But that didn't really work."

Not a threat. I think I actually snorted when I read that. "I'm not a threat," I typed angrily. "I only contemplated murdering you four times today!" I hit send and slammed my laptop shut. Carter and I had been "friends" for less than twenty-four hours and I was already regretting the decision to be friends with him again. He was lying through his teeth (well, in this case, his fingers) to me, and expected me to just take it because we were friends. Well I wasn't having it. Not one word of it.

I pushed myself out of my desk chair, pulled out my copy of To Kill a Mockingbird out of my backpack, and began my reading assignment.

Carter Greenspan: A name at Lincoln High synonymous with douche.

"So Carter messaged me last night," I told Willow between bites of yogurt in the cafeteria the next morning.

"Oh yeah?" Willow asked, examining her fingernails.

"Yeah, he told me that he only called me 'just Violet' so that Anna wouldn't think of me as competition, even though apparently I am."

"He said you would be competition for Anna? That's ridiculous," she said, looking up from her fingernails.

See, even Willow thought it was ridiculous that anyone would think that I could possibly compete with Anna Ryan.

"I didn't let him get to that part, but that's definitely where he was headed."

Just then, Carter came into the cafeteria and sat right in my line of site. I glared at him while scraping the bottom of my yogurt container with my spoon. Likely noticing my dirty looks, he took it upon himself to come over to my table.

"Hello Violet, Willow," he said giving us each a nod as he took a seat. Willow gave him a sarcastic wave while I remained silent.

"Vi, I know you're mad," he said quietly. "But I want you to know I was being serious about everything I said last night and I really do want to be friends."

"I don't know if I want to be friends with someone who is going to lie to me. Especially considering this is your second chance. In case you've forgotten, we used to be best friends and you screwed that up too," I said in one breath.

"Vi, I didn't lie. And I'm truly sorry about everything that happened in middle school. I really am. Can you find it in your heart to forgive me? Please?" he pleaded, nervously running his hand through his sandy hair.

"Okay, I forgive you," I said. "Now we can go back to pretending we don't know each other."

"I don't want that," he said plainly.

"How come no one is taking into consideration what I want?" I asked, beginning to get angry.

"Well, is that what you want?" he asked.

"At this point it seems like the best option."

Carter sighed. "Vi, I didn't lie."

"If I believed you, we'd both be wrong," I told him as the bell rang, indicating that it was time to go to class. I picked up my backpack and stormed out of the cafeteria for first period.

My first two classes went by, relatively annoyance free, but when I got to third period I pulled out my phone and saw that I had a new picture message from Carter. I opened it, unsure of what to expect. The picture was of my keys and the caption said "Need these?"

"Of course I need those, you moron," I replied.

"Obviously they're not that important if you forgot them," he said.

"I was in a hurry. Some asshole wouldn't leave me alone."

"Ouch. Why do you have to be like that, Vi?"

"Be like what? I'm just being myself. I'm not the sweet little 12 year-old I was the last time you gave me the time of day." I hit send before realizing that might have been a little harsh.

"Well, looks like you're missing your keys and that asshole might have to give you a ride home," said his reply.

"Why would I get a ride from him? Willow could drive me."

"Because he lives on the same street as you, whereas Willow lives on the other side of town."

He had a point. Riding with him would make the most economical sense, although if he would just give me my keys back I wouldn't need to get a ride with anyone. But that probably wouldn't happen because he was so damn persistent.

Lunch came and went and the rest of my classes followed suit. By the end of the day I was still keyless and so desperate to get them back that I resorted to tracking Carter down in the hall. Luckily, he was at the first place I checked, his locker.

I tapped him once on the shoulder and as he turned around I put my hand out. "Can I please have my keys?" I asked in the sweetest voice I could muster, hoping he would be reminded of the child version of me that he had been best friends with.

Carter smiled. "Tell you what, Vi. I'll give you your keys if you promise to hang out with me soon."

"Why do you want to hang out with me so bad?" I asked, exasperatedly, dropping my arm in near defeat.

He looked down, almost sadly. "I just miss being such good friends, Violet. I miss it. I miss you."

"I think we've established that you don't really know me anymore."

"Let's change that," he said simply.

My head was spinning. Somehow I had landed in an alternate universe, but I didn't even remember the twister. "I have a feeling we're not in Kansas anymore," I mumbled under my breath.

"What was that?" Carter asked, looking from the ground to me.

"I'll think about it," I said, grabbing my keys out of his hand. With that, I marched back down the hall, out of the building, to my car and drove over to Trudi's apartment.

I mean what I say. Usually.

I walked into my aunt's apartment where she was sitting on the couch watching a rerun of The Golden Girls. "Oh, hey, you're here," she noted as I walked in and set my stuff down.

"Yeah, well I almost wasn't," I said, dropping down on the couch next to her.

"What do you mean?" she asked, giving me a puzzled look as she turned off the television.

"Carter took my keys this morning and didn't give them back until I basically ripped them out of his hand after school. He tried to make me swear to hang out with him," I added.

"Well?" she asked, looking impatient.

"Well what?" I asked back.

"When are you going to hang out with him?" She had an eager look in her eye.

"I told him I would think about it," I said. "I don't want to, at all, but I guess I'll have to if I want him to leave me alone."

"Don't do that!" Trudi nearly shouted, taking me by surprise. "You can't just give in like that!"

"Three seconds ago you were going to tell me that I should hang out with him," I pointed out.

"Well I changed my mind," she said with a pensive look on her face. "Do you remember when you were kids, how you and Carter would come over here while your moms were at yoga class Wednesday afternoons?"

"Yeah, sure?" I said, nodding. I wasn't sure where she as going with this or why this was relevant.

"Well there was one time when you ran into the apartment screaming that Carter was hurt outside, so I went out to see what was wrong and he had scraped his knee on the pavement. I asked what happened and he said he fell down while he was chasing you," she said raising an eyebrow at me as if this was supposed to magically give me some insight.

"Yeah, I'm sure that happened," I said, coaxing her to continue.

"After I finished cleaning Carter up and getting Band-Aids on him, I told him that he shouldn't chase you anymore if he didn't want to get hurt, and do you know what he said to me?"

"No, Trudi, I don't. That was eleven years ago."

"He said to me 'But girls are meant to be chased,'" she said.

"Can you get to the point?" I asked impatiently. Trudi, of all people, should know that I hated drawn out explanations.

"That's the point, Violet! You can't see it?!"

"Apparently not."

"Make him remember that girls are meant to be chased. That *you're* meant to be chased," she urged.

Although I felt like the notion was sort of objectifying, I was actually impressed. Was it possible that my aunt had just given me almost decent advice that didn't end in a story about chlamydia? I sat there for a bit, not really sure of how to react to this change of suit my aunt had. For starters, I wouldn't give her the satisfaction of thinking that I agreed with her.

"So that's all I'm good for?" I asked. "Being chased?"

"No, but it will make it much more satisfying for the both of you."

"Who says I'm not satisfied?!" I asked angrily.

"Your tone."

"I don't even know how to *make* him chase me, you know?" I said nervously.

"Well you have to be yourself," she reminded me. "Don't change who you are over a boy. Don't give in just because he is who he is. He has to know his birthright hasn't given him an advantage. But most importantly, be irresistible."

"If I knew how to be irresistible I wouldn't be in a situation like this," I said pointedly.

"That's not the point," Trudi said with a glare. She hated hearing me talk negatively about myself. "Guys want what they can't have. If you let him think he can have you, he wins. If you don't give in he'll have to chase you because he won't give up without a fight. But don't do anything that doesn't feel right to you."

"He *can't* have me," I told her.

"You know what I mean, Violet. Your friendship!"

I was completely flabbergasted by the entire conversation. My aunt never gave good advice, but here she was all Dear Abby and I wasn't sure how to react at all.

"Who are you and what have you done with my aunt?" I asked with a small chuckle.

After having such a good conversation, which included real advice, I decided I shouldn't press my luck with my aunt anymore. I went home and went straight to my room, choosing to forgo dinner for this evening. We were having pork chops, and I didn't really like pork anyway.

I opened my laptop and logged on to Facebook. The only worthwhile notification was a wallpost from Willow, outlining our Anti-Prom plans. "Prom is in one month, so I've taken the liberty of planning what we're going to do that night. I've devised a playlist of John Hughes movies and am making a snack list. Let me know if there's anything in particular you want. ☺"

What was more was that there was a comment from Carter that said "Why aren't you going to prom?"

"It's just not our thing," Willow had responded.

"That sounds great, Willow. Make sure you get something peanut butter! ;)" I commented, not dignifying Carter's comment with a response.

***

Saturday morning I sat in my bed reading when I got a text from Carter. "Do you have plans tonight?"

"No," I typed. Before I hit send, I remembered what my aunt said about not caving in. I erased what I had typed and sent instead, "Yeah, I do."

Not even a minute later his response came. "What are you doing?"

"Sex, drugs and rock and roll. What does anyone do on a Saturday night?"

"Lol, for real though?" he texted back.

"If it concerned you, you would already know about it," I told him. After that I got out of bed, got dressed and went downstairs for breakfast. My mother usually insisted on eating breakfast as a family on Saturday mornings, and since I skipped dinner the night before, I felt like I should comply.

I sat down at the table and helped myself to the French toast that had already been set out. After everyone was settled in and had begun to eat, my mother decided to make a big announcement that I felt was mostly directed toward me. "Linda Greenspan invited us to a barbecue at their house after church tomorrow. Doesn't that sound like fun?"

"Oh, but since I don't go to church, I assume I'm not included in those plans?" I asked hopefully.

"Don't be ridiculous, Violet," my mother said. Somehow she always had a way of putting extra emphasis on my name to make things sound menacing. "You will go along with the rest of the family. And please, wear something *nice*."

I groaned loudly. Unfortunately for me, my mother's idea of nice meant I should dress like a housewife in the 1950's. Fortunately for my mother, she had bought me a new outfit for me to wear to church twice a month for the past two years. Let me point out that the last time I went to church I was friends with Carter.

After breakfast, I opened up my closet and spread out the section of clothes I referred to as "Church Clothes." My mother had bought me all these clothes in an attempt to coax me out of my "rebellious phase," which I don't feel is an appropriate term for this "phase" in my life, which wasn't really a phase, and the only act of rebellion I committed was not going to church.

I never felt that having differing beliefs from my parents made me all that rebellious, since other than that I (mostly) followed the rules set for me. But once my mother made up her mind about something, there was no changing it.

I sighed in defeat as I shut my closet door. I didn't really feel like going through clothes I never wanted to wear to find an outfit to wear to a barbecue I didn't want to go to. I decided to check Facebook, although I was getting slightly annoyed with my reliance on Facebook to ease my boredom. As I scrolled through the newsfeed, one thing caught my eye. It was a status update Carter has posted about fifteen minutes earlier that said "Excited for tomorrow! ☺"

I rolled my eyes and noticed that it didn't feel like I was straining my eye muscles anymore. I posted a status that said "Not excited for tomorrow. I'm tired of my mom forcing me to do things I don't want to do." I shut my laptop and began getting ready for work.

I got to work and luckily Willow was working with me that day. It really helped to have a friend during the slow periods so I would have someone to talk to. We had been at work for about an hour when Willow pointed to something across the food court. There, sitting at a table near the Wendy's stand was Anna and Kevin Davis sharing a milkshake.

"That was fast," I said.

"Not really, considering Carter had moved on before they were even broken up," Willow said, raising an eyebrow at me.

"What are you talking about?" I asked, although I knew what she meant. She was trying to tell me Carter liked me, which I'm sure wasn't even near true.

Willow stared at me for a second. "Are you really that blind, Violet?" she asked. "The dude showed up at your house at three in the morning to as if you can *be friends*. And the next day he and his girlfriend break up over it. How does that not have anything to do with you?"

I paused to consider this before making my argument. "I don't really think Carter actually wanted to be friends with me. I think his mom has something to do with it. I think she told him he needs to be friends with me to make things easier on her and my mom. She invited us to a barbecue at their house tomorrow."

"Are you going?" Willow asked in surprise.

"I have to. My mother won't let me get out of it," I said, annoyance apparent in my voice.

"Oh… Good luck," she said with a smirk.

"I'm going to avoid him at all costs," I said calmly.

Typical family barbecue. If you grew up in the Bundy family.

There was a knock at my door, pulling me out of a relatively peaceful sleep. "What?" I groaned at the closed door.

"Violet, are you sure you don't want to go to church?" my mother called through the wood.

"Positive," I confirmed.

"Honey, I really wish you would just come to church with the family. Please?"

"Mom," I began my argument. "I am not going to church. I haven't gone to church in more than three years and I'm not going to start now. If I'm going to be forced to go to the Greenspan's barbecue, I am not going to let you talk me into going to church."

"If that's how you're going to be." I could picture the look on her face as she said it. Seconds later, I heard her walk down the stairs.

I remained in bed until I heard the car doors shut and my family leave for church. I got up and opened my closet in an attempt to find the least hideous "nice" outfit that I owned.

I picked out a mid-thigh length lavender pencil skirt with a white shirt and matching lavender sweater. I pulled them on, which was hard, considering I was trying not to throw up on them. I smoothed the skirt and adjusted my sweater.

I walked over to my vanity and started working on my hair and makeup, thoughts of what Willow had said the night before echoed in my mind. I had just put the finishing touches on my appearance, which was more for my mother than anyone else, when she called up the stairs that it was time to go.

I walked downstairs and into the kitchen where my mom was rushing around getting things ready to go down the street. "You look nice, honey," she stated when she saw me.

"Thanks," I muttered, unconvinced.

"You need to carry this," she said, handing me a giant bowl of potato salad and practically shoving me out the door. "Get going, we're going to be late," she urged.

I wasn't sure why my mother was always so concerned with impressing the Greenspans. Mrs. Greenspan was her best friend. I had never felt the desire to compete with either best friend I'd had throughout my life, which I guess proved that I hadn't inherited my mother's competitive nature. Though there were times when I wasn't sure I had inherited anything from either of my parents.

I walked down the street and pushed through the gate at the Greenspan's house, letting myself into the backyard. It was exactly the same as it had been years ago when I was there last.

As I set the potato salad on the table that held the rest of the food, I felt someone behind me. Unexpectedly, someone whispered in my ear. "You're awfully dressed up for someone who hasn't been to church in months."

"Years, actually," I said turning around to face Carter, still dressed in his church clothes. "And if I had my way I wouldn't be here either," I added.

He stared at me for a brief moment, as if contemplating whether or not to believe me. He opened his mouth to respond, but before he could say anything he was interrupted.

"Carter, could you go in the house and get some ice?" Mrs. Greenspan called from across the yard. Carter turned and walked into the house leaving me alone. Finally. I decided to use my solitude to take a lap around the yard. I walked past Liana, Daniel and Carter's sister Nina playing tag and eventually settled on the very same swing I had dreamt about just a few nights previous.

I was sitting on the swing for a few minutes before Carter walked out again. I couldn't help but imagine what life would be like if he had remained friends all that time, which is a thought I hadn't had since middle school. I looked at Carter and noticed that he was relatively attractive, not that it hadn't crossed my mind before. Even though I was still angry with him, that didn't make him any less attractive. I couldn't help but question the alternate future we would have had if it weren't for Anna. Would I have ended up being Carter's girlfriend?

I pushed the thought from my mind before I could get attached to it and reminded myself of what an ass he had been the past week. I still couldn't believe how he had been acting. At that moment, Carter made eye contact and walked toward me. *Crap*, I thought to myself. I sighed loudly as he approached.

"Don't act so excited to see me, Vi," he remarked.

"I'll try to contain my enthusiasm," I said sarcastically.

"You know, we used to be friends."

"Used to, being the operative phrase," I pointed out. "Need I remind you it's your fault we're not friends anymore?"

"No, I already know that," he conceded. "But I was thirteen, and I was an idiot."

"Yeah, and now you're seventeen and you're still an idiot," I reminded him.

"Maybe I am, but I'm trying, Vi," he said.

"Not trying hard enough," I pointed out.

"What more could I possibly do?"

"Oh, I don't know. Stop being a dick, maybe."

He stared at me for a moment, a genuine look of hurt in his eye. "Vi…" he started. It was obvious he didn't know what to say. "I am sorry, okay? I want to make it up to you. I honestly regret just going away like that."

"Well that was your mistake," I said cockily, remembering what Trudi said about not giving in. I got up off the swing and walked toward our parents who were starting to serve the younger kids.

I sat next to Daniel who was suffering from a severe case of what we liked to call "Big Boy Syndrome," and insisted on cutting his own steak .After a few successful knife strokes, his hand slipped and his knife went straight for Nina's arm. Luckily, I caught his hand before he stabbed Nina, saving our families from any more potential scars caused by one child to another. Although in this case it would have been a physical scar.

***

The next morning, I walked into the cafeteria and sat down with Willow. After some small talk, Willow discreetly pointed across the cafeteria to where Carter was sitting alone.

"Is there something wrong with him?" she asked. "How was yesterday?"

"Oh, well…" I began, unsure of where to actually begin. "I basically told him that he needs to stop trying because he already messed up and I don't really want to be friends with him. And I may or may not have called him a dick."

"Oh, so you're the reason for his emo-fest?" she asked, raising an eyebrow.

"I wouldn't say that," I said. "He should have figured it out a long time ago, when I stopped trying to get him to be my friend. I don't care that we aren't friends anymore. I'm not going to change my mind because he bats his eyelashes at me and tries to play the charm card. It's not going to work with me."

Willow stared at me as if she found my logic completely bogus. "Why are you treating him like shit?" she asked.

"What? You wouldn't?"

"Vi, you've known him your entire life, and he's giving you the time of day for the first time since middle school and you're treating him like absolute crap."

"Exactly," I argued. "I've known him my entire life, and he is speaking to me again for the first time since middle school. He completely ignored me for FOUR years. And either way, I'm not going to let him win without a fight."

After a couple of minutes the bell rang and I got up to go to class. Once in the classroom, I threw my stuff down on a desk and settled in. As I sat down, I felt my phone buzz against my hip. I slipped it out of my pocket and looked at the screen. I had a new message from Carter.

"Can we have lunch together today?" he had said.

"Can you take a hint?" I responded.

"It doesn't look like it."

"When are you going to realize that I'm not just another high school girl who's going to fall all over you just because you're hot?" I asked him.

"Well at least now I know you think I'm hot," he said, and I could just imagine the smirk he was wearing on his face somewhere inside this building.

"That's exactly my point," I said, not bothering to add that he knew he was hot and acted like a jerk about it.

"Miss Montgomery," said the voice of Mrs. Avery, my biology teacher. "Can you put the phone away so I can begin my class?"

I complied embarrassedly, sliding the phone back into my pocket and not taking it out again when I felt the vibration indicating Carter's response. I sat through class impatiently, wanting to know what it said. When the bell finally rang and I was able to look at my phone again, all he had said was "Hear me out."

"Fine," I replied.

Willow and I met up in the hallway and walked to our next class, which luckily we had together.

"I'm going to need to share your book with you today," I told her.

"Why?" she asked.

"I'm afraid to open my locker," I stated. "Carter might be hiding inside it."

My next two classes went by ridiculously fast, because I was dreading what was coming next.

After third period, I sent Willow a message that said that I had agreed to meet Carter for lunch and that I would see her afterward.

I sat down at an empty table in the cafeteria, and luckily Carter didn't keep me waiting long.

"Talk," I said as soon as he arrived at the table.

He sighed and sat down. After a few prolonged seconds, he finally spoke. "Violet, I'm really sorry I messed things up," he said. "I have been trying to fix things but apparently my efforts aren't really having the desired effect."

I had to hand it to Carter; he definitely didn't fit the 'jock' stereotype as well as anyone would think. His vocabulary and use of proper grammar made it difficult to stay angry with him. However, I didn't want to be played the fool, and I wasn't entirely convinced of his sincerity, so I decided to continue to stand my ground.

"You did mess it up," I agreed. "And it took four years for you to try to fix it. And then when you tried to fix it you messed it up again the next day. Forgive me for not thinking that you're actually trying here." It was apparent that I was angry with him.

"You don't understand," he said sadly, looking down at his hands which were fidgeting on the table.

"You're not doing a very good job of making me understand," I pointed out.

He sighed gain and stared at me for a brief moment. "Do you think I would just show up at someone's house in the middle of the night if the reason I was there wasn't important?" he asked.

"That's not what I'd like to think, but your resulting actions somehow contradicted the actions previous."

He stared at me, seemingly appalled. "Why are you doing this to me?"

"Doing what to you?" I asked, genuinely confused. I was doing nothing to him. He was doing it all to me. I was definitely not the one in the wrong in this situation.

"Making me regret every decision I've made in the last four years," he said, as if I should have already known that was what he meant.

"They were your decisions," I reminded him with a shrug.

"They were stupid decisions," he said.

"I can't say I disagree," I told him. "But they were decisions you made."

"Vi, I don't want you to think that I don't care about you," he said. "You're still really important to me. I feel terrible about what I did, and I don't know what else I can do to prove that to you."

Maybe I was being a little hard on the kid. But what was I supposed to do? How was I supposed to believe that he suddenly wanted to be my friend for absolutely no apparent reason after years of not speaking? How was I supposed to be sure that he wouldn't just hurt me all over again?

"Try a little harder," I advised him, standing up and turning to walk away. Before I left I turned back to him and added "And don't bother continuing to apologize. It's getting annoying."

A lie never hurt anyone, right?
RIGHT?!!?!

The next two classes dragged on almost at half speed. I had no desire to be at school under normal circumstance, but that day I would have rather been trampled on by stampeding wildebeests than spend the rest of the day in school. When the bell finally rang at the end of the day, I got to my car as fast as humanly possible, trying my best to avoid seeing Carter in the hallway and having to talk to him.

I got home and walked into the kitchen where my mother was sitting at the counter filling out some paperwork. "How was your day?" she asked, not looking up from her papers. Typical for my mother, to pretend to care.

Just as I opened my mouth to tell her that I didn't have the best day, Liana ran into the room. "MOM! I need you to come help me with something!" she screamed.

My mother got up and followed Liana out of the room without even acknowledging the fact that she hadn't let me speak. The fact that this was a regular occurrence left me unperturbed.

I walked up the stairs to my room and fed Pudge. I stared at him for a little while, mesmerized by how smoothly he glided through the water. Next I sat down at my desk and pulled out my algebra book.

After almost forty-five minutes of math homework, I got bored and decided to get on Facebook. I did my customary scroll through all the unimportant posts until something Carter posted caught my eye.

"Kicking myself for screwing things up, but I'm determined to fix this," his status said. Anna Ryan liked the status, no doubt assuming it was about her. However that possibility was put to reset in the comments.

Jeff Williams commented and said "U tlkn about Anna?"

"Nope. Someone much more important," was Carter's resulting comment.

I closed out of Facebook and shut my laptop. "At least he took what I said seriously," I said aloud to myself.

That night as I was drifting off to sleep, I got a text message from Carter saying "Goodnight, Vi."

"Night," was all I texted back.

***

The next three days were completely uneventful. Carter texted me a few times but was surprisingly very casual about it. He didn't insist that we spend time together or try to make me feel guilty for not wanting to hang out. That is until Thursday after school.

"Hey, a few of us are going camping Saturday night. Join us?" said the text he had sent me.

"I'll think about it," I told him.

"It's going to be a lot of fun! I promise," he said.

"I'll let you know," I said. Next I texted Willow telling her to meet me at Trudi's immediately.

Once I got to Trudi's I paced the kitchen waiting for Willow to get there while Trudi made the three of us tea.

"Vi, what's wrong?" Trudi asked.

"Nothing," I muttered.

"Don't give me that. You're going to wear a hole in my floor," she told me. "What is wrong?"

"Just wait for Willow to get here so I can tell you both at once!" I snapped.

Trudi complied, knowing there was no point in trying to force it out of me now and making me repeat it for Willow.

After a few more minutes of my stressed pacing of my aunt's kitchen, Willow walked through the door and sat down at the table. I threw my phone on the table so they could read the message from Carter.

My aunt squealed upon reading the message. "Our plan is working!"

Willow glared at Trudi before turning to me. "Do you really think it's a good idea, Vi?" she asked.

"I don't know," I said with a sigh, sitting down at the table. "I mean, I'm tired of treating him like crap, and it does sound like fun, but what if it's a set up?"

"How could it be a set up?!" Trudi asked, as if she too thought Carter was the greatest thing ever.

"Oh, let's see... A bunch of guys in the woods with one girl," I said. "How could that possibly be a setup?"

Trudi rolled her eyes at me and took a sip of her tea. "You just need to trust him, Vi," she told me. "He's not a bad guy."

"I know he's not a bad guy," I conceded. "But that doesn't mean he won't do something that his friends tell him is a good idea even if it really isn't."

"Vi, I don't think he'll really do anything you wouldn't want," Willow pointed out. "I know that most of his friends are idiots, but I don't think he's dumb enough to make you do anything that will make you uncomfortable."

I stared at Willow in disbelief. "He's been making me uncomfortable for two weeks," I pointed out.

"You know what I mean though," she said. "Vi, he hasn't done anything *harmful* to you. He hasn't done anything to hurt you, really. And isn't that what you're worried about."

I hadn't really thought about it, but maybe she had a point. I didn't know what I was worried about, but I knew I was worried. Could it have been that deep down I was worried he was going to hurt me? I sighed, admitting defeat and pulled my phone toward me, not sure of what I was going to do.

I looked from Willow to Trudi and back again, searching their faces for answers. "I don't want to go camping alone with a bunch of dudes though," I admitted.

Willow grabbed my phone out of my hand and started typing. When she was finished she held the phone in her hand, not giving it back to me. I didn't attempt to get it from her because I knew if I had it in my hand I would have to give Carter an answer.

My phone beeped and Willow opened the text message that had just come. She smiled as she read it, and then handed the phone to me. It was from Carter and said "Of course. I was actually going to suggest you invite her anyway."

I raised an eyebrow at Willow and looked at the previous message she had sent. "Can Willow come?"

I looked over at her and smiled. I knew that she wouldn't want to go camping with a bunch of guys she wasn't friends with, but was glad she was willing to anyway. Trudi snatched my phone out of my hand and read the messages.

"Make sure you're both wearing cute underwear!" she told us.

Willow stared at her for a good four seconds. "Why?" she asked.

Willow and Trudi had an odd sort of relationship. They both really liked each other but they butted heads nearly constantly. Willow wasn't passive about letting my aunt know that her advice wasn't necessarily appreciated. Willow was also very set in her ways and wouldn't do anything she didn't want to just because someone told her she should.

"Well you never know if anyone is going to see them," Trudi said. Her intentions were good, I'm sure, but she definitely underestimated the amount of pressure it would take to get Willow or I to be put in a compromising situation.

"We'll be fine, Trudi," I said, hoping to quell the issue before it got out of hand.

"I'm serious," she persisted. "Do you need me to buy you anything? You know, to stay safe?"

"Oh my god, Trudi! Neither of us is going to be having sex this weekend!" I shouted across the table at her.

"Trust me girls," she said, causing both Willow and I to roll our eyes. "You never know when it's gonna happen. You need to be prepared. You're going to be out in the woods with boys overnight. Don't tell me that they're not expecting something."

"You were the one who was just telling me that I should trust Carter," I pointed out. "And now you're telling me that he's going to try to take advantage of me?"

"I'm just saying that you need to be realistic," she said calmly.

"We'll be fine," I assured her. "We know how to stand our ground."

Trudi threw her arms up in defeat. "Fine! If you don't want my advice, I won't give it."

"I've been waiting to hear her say that for years," Willow said, laughing.

"Trudi, can you please not take everything so personally?" I asked. I was starting to get annoyed that she kept getting so hurt about us not taking her advice when the advice wasn't necessarily applicable.

As we left Trudi's house Willow agreed to come over the next afternoon to help me pack for the camping trip. We both left and went to our separate homes.

Friday morning, I sat in my usual spot in the cafeteria while Carter sat in his usual spot across the cafeteria. He made eye contact with me and smiled, but I pretended to care too much about the pen I was twirling between my fingers to notice.

After a while, he and the group of guys surrounding him got up and walked out of the cafeteria. As they passed my table on the way out, Carter looked back at me and said "See you tomorrow," with a wink.

I rolled my eyes blatantly and saw him smirk at me over his shoulder. I definitely wasn't going to let him get the better of me. I was going to play it off like I was only going on this camping trip to get him to leave me alone, which was mostly true. Sure, I may have been attracted to Carter, but he was never going to know it.

The rest of the day went by without anything excited happening. Although Anna Ryan gave me death glares every time she saw me. Maybe she had heard that Carter invited me camping. Or maybe that was just her face.

Willow and I went to my house after school to start packing. We walked into the house to find my mother and the kids in the kitchen working on their homework. Upon seeing them, I remembered one tiny detail. I forgot to get my parents' permission for this little camping trip. Since I knew my mom wouldn't be too keen on letting me go camping with a bunch of boys, I decided to fudge the truth a little bit.

I opened the fridge and examined the contents on the shelves, knowing this would work a lot better if my mother wasn't looking at me when I said it. "Umm, Mom. I'm going camping with Willow tomorrow night, okay?" I said, with my face still in the fridge.

It wasn't exactly a lie. Willow would be there. I just didn't specify who else would be there.

"That sounds lovely, honey," my mother said. Luckily for me, I could rarely count on my mother to pay too much attention to anything I told her. I turned to leave the kitchen, and as I walked out, she caught me off guard by saying something else. "Do you want me to call Mrs. Phan and ask if there is anything you need to bring?"

I stopped short. Crap. What was I going to tell her? Luckily, Willow beat me to it.

"That's not necessary, Mrs. Montgomery," she said. "We already have everything we need. Vi just needs to bring her personal stuff." She smiled sincerely at my mother before turning and walking up the stairs toward my room.

"Are you sure?" my mother called after us. "I could call her to make sure it's no trouble for you to go." I stopped walking.

"It's fine, Mom," I called back down the stairs. "Mrs. Phan invited me herself."

"Okay, have fun then," she said.

I ran the rest of the way up the stairs and joined Willow in my bedroom. Lying always made me ridiculously nervous.

"What did you tell your parents?" I asked Willow when I got to my room.

"What do you mean?" Willow asked.

Sometimes I forgot how different mine and Willow's home lives were. Her parents were super laid back and didn't really care what she did as long as she told them before-hand. So she probably did tell them that she was going camping with a bunch of boys, and they were probably perfectly okay with it.

Oh, never mind," I said. "But obviously my mother assumes your parents are going with us."

"My parents are going to be in Sacramento at Julia's house anyway," Willow said. Julia was one of Willow's older sisters, who was married and had a flock of children. Her parents went to visit them at least twice a month.

"And you're bringing the tent, right?" I asked, making sure we had everything covered.

"What else do I need?" I asked. I had never been camping before. I obviously understood the basics, but I didn't know what to bring and I didn't want to look like an idiot.

"You need some pajamas, obviously," she said.

I looked in the drawer where I kept my pajamas, unsure of which ones to bring. I knew I shouldn't care about appearances, especially for sleeping in the woods, but I was still being really picky about it. I settled on some grey Hollister sweatpants and a purple long sleeve shirt. I brought them back to my bed and put them in the bag that I planned on using.

"Okay what else?"

"What are you wearing tomorrow?" Willow asked.

I stopped and stared at her. "I don't know," I said after a few seconds.

Willow laughed. "Wear shorts and a t-shirt because it's supposed to be hot," she said. "And then you need to bring some warmer clothes for later in the day when it starts to cool down. Jeans and a sweatshirt."

I nodded and opened up my closet to find jeans and a hoodie, which I also stuffed in my bag.

"And then you need shorts and another t-shirt to wear Sunday," she said.

Once all the clothes I would need were in my bag, I started gathering toiletries. I put my toothbrush, toothpaste, hair brush, shampoo, conditioner, body wash and deodorant in my bag. "Anything else?" I asked Willow, who eyed my bag.

"I think that's it," she said.

"Perfect," I said. Willow and I walked to the front door together. "I'll see you tomorrow," I said as she left.

I went back to my room and picked up my phone. There was a message that was more than an hour old from Carter. "See you tomorrow," was all it said.

I spent the night unpacking and repacking my bag, thinking about what my aunt Trudi had said. I didn't want to assume the worst of Carter, but I really shouldn't assume that he had the best of intentions either. I knew that I was good at standing my ground but I was worried that he might actually be able to charm the pants off of me. Literally.

I sighed and moved to my dresser. I dug through the top drawer and found my cutest pair of underwear and matching bra, and set them on top of my bag. "Just in case," I whispered to myself. I got into bed and went to sleep.

Because everyone knows that sunset is best experienced from the edge of a cliff.

The next morning, I took my stuff out to my car and told my parents I was leaving. They gave me the usual "Be careful, don't wander off into the woods, eat your vegetables," speech.

The plan we had devised was that I would pick up Willow and take her to Carter's house and then we would take my car as well as someone else's car so that mine or Willow's car wouldn't stay at Carter's house for the night because my parents would definitely notice that.

I picked up Willow and we put her stuff in my car and drove over to Carter's house, going the long way around so we wouldn't have to pass my house. Everyone was already at Carter's house and we decided who would ride in which car. It was decided that Carter, Liam and Willow would ride in my car, while Tyler, Steven and Jeff rode in Tyler's girlfriend, Erin's car.

Once we were all in the car and ready to go, we pulled out and drove toward the campsite. Somehow Carter ended up in the passenger seat and Willow got stuck in the backseat with Liam, which I'm sure he didn't mind.

After Carter spent five minutes messing with my radio, he finally found a station that was playing modern hits. A Katy Perry song came on and we all sang along, laughing. Liam and Carter talked about baseball, but Willow and I were quiet, because I was focusing on following Erin, and we didn't really want to have to try talking over the guys.

"Dude, remember the last time we went camping here?" Liam asked when we approached the sign that said we were five miles from the campsite.

"Yeah," Carter said. "There were a bunch of nudists about three spots over," he told Willow and me, with a laugh.

Willow laughed but I was unsure of whether or not this was a common thing.

"What's wrong, Violet?" Liam asked, noticing how quiet I was.

"Nothing," I said.

"Hmm, sure?" Liam asked. I thought it was nice that he was concerned about me.

"She's never been camping," Willow informed them. "But I told her it's nothing to worry about."

Carter let out a small chuckle. "Are you scared, Vi?"

"I'm not scared," I told him. "I already said I don't know what to expect."

"I'm alright," I promised.

"Don't worry," Liam said. "We'll protect you." He playfully punched Carter on the arm.

I looked over to Carter and wondered if there was a double meaning in that statement. Did Carter have a plan for tonight that I didn't know about? And if he did, did Liam know about it? Did everyone know about it except for me? I pushed the thoughts out of my head and decided that this trip needed to be fun, and I should try not to let my paranoia get me down.

We pulled into the campgrounds and drove around looking for a campsite. When we found two together, Erin asked Willow and I to go with her to pay for them while the guys unloaded our stuff. I opened my trunk so that they could get the stuff out of it, and the three of us walked toward the campground offices.

"This is your first time camping?" Erin asked me. I didn't really know Erin but she seemed nice.

"Yeah," I admitted. "I'm actually pretty excited."

"It's a lot of fun," Erin said. "And I'm glad you two are here. Usually I'm the only girl, which kind of sucks. One time Anna came and all she did was complain about things being dirty, which was *really* annoying." She rolled her eyes.

Willow and I laughed. It was apparent that Erin didn't like Anna, which gave us something in common, at least.

"Besides, I think you're a lot better for Carter than Anna was," she said smiling.

I stopped walking. "What do you mean?" Maybe Carter did have a plan that I didn't know about.

Erin stared at me briefly. "Well it's obvious that Carter has it bad for you. And I think he sort of thought that by agreeing to come tonight you might reciprocate those feelings..." she said the last part quietly.

I bit my bottom lip and looked at the ground.

"She does," Willow said. "She just won't admit it to herself or anyone else."

"That's not true!" I nearly shouted. "If I did have feelings for him I would be able to admit it to myself at the very least."

Willow stared at me knowingly. "Don't even try, Vi."

"Carter has about as much of a chance of getting with me as Liam has of getting with you," I told her.

Willow shrugged. "Liam isn't that bad."

I threw my arms up in defeat. "Does Carter have some sort of plan that I don't know about?" I demanded.

Erin shrugged. "I don't think he really has a plan," she said. "He was so surprised that you even agreed to go, I don't think he could have come up with a plan even if he wanted to."

I shook my head. I didn't even know what to make of the situation. Trudi and Willow had tried to tell me that his intentions weren't just to be friends again but for some reason it didn't make sense until Erin said it. Once again, I decided to just enjoy my first camping trip and not let it get to me.

"Whatever," I said with a shrug.

We approached the campground office and Erin told the attendant which campsites we were at and paid for both of them.

"Why do we need two?" I asked when we walked away from the office. "They looked pretty big."

"Once you put the tents up, there's not a lot of room, so we get one to put our tents in and then we hang out in the other one. We're not going to hang out in the tents the whole time," Erin explained, smiling.

"Duh," I said. I decided that if I had any more questions about camping I would just ask Willow in private.

We got back to the campsite where all the guys were setting up tents. There was one for Tyler and Erin, one for Jeff and Steven and one for Carter and Liam. Willow brought one for the two of us, but no one had begun setting it up.

Willow opened the tent bag and began pulling the parts out almost at the same time that Liam had pulled out his and Carter's tent.

"Willow, do you even know how to set up a tent?" Liam asked, eyebrow raised, with a smirk on his face.

"I hope I can manage," Willow said, a faux dumbstruck look spreading across her face. She started snapping the poles together and setting our tent up. After about five minutes our tent was up and ready to go, while Carter and Liam were still struggling with their tent. "Need help?" Willow asked cockily.

"No thanks," Liam said with a grin. "We're men. We're perfectly capable of setting up a tent."

"Whatever you say," Willow said, taking a seat next to Erin and me on the picnic table. We laughed as we watched Carter and Liam argue over which poles went where.

Once all the tents were finally up, all five guys came and lifted the table that the three of us girls were sitting on and carried it to the other campsite. We all laughed along the ride. I was thoroughly impressed that they were able to carry the table with all three of us on it, but decided not to give them the satisfaction of knowing that.

We spent a few hours sitting at the campsite, eating hotdogs and talking and laughing. I was having a great time, surprisingly enough. Carter wasn't really bothering me, and Willow looked like she was having fun too. Overall, I was glad I had decided to go. It definitely beat spending the night at home.

Around 7 o'clock, Carter asked if anyone wanted to go for a hike. I said yes, but everyone else stayed quiet.

"Come on guys!" Carter urged, but no one really seemed enthused.

I was slightly irritated that no one else wanted to go, but since I wasn't letting anything affect my good mood, I decided not to care.

"Do you still want to go, Vi?" Carter asked, looking hopeful.

I couldn't say no, because he would know it was because I didn't want to be alone with him, so I agreed anyway.

We set off down a trail near the edge of our campsite. We followed the trail down about half a mile, taking different forks at random. I knew Carter and the rest of the guys had been camping here, so I assumed he had been on this trail before and followed his lead.

We followed various trails for around forty-five minutes until we emerged into a clearing on the edge of a cliff. There were flowers blooming, and wild clover scattered throughout the grass. It was a really beautiful scene.

Carter pointed to the west where the sun was setting. I would be lying if I said it wasn't one of the most amazing sunsets I had ever seen. The bright orange near the horizon made it look as if the sky were on fire. The wispy clouds were a magnificent shade of pink and above our heads was a shade of purple that made everything else look almost dull.

I wondered why we were here. Was this part of the plan that Carter apparently hadn't made but everyone other than me seemed to know about? I looked over at him and he was still staring at the sunset.

"It's really pretty out here," I said, deciding to compliment the place he brought me to before I questioned his motives.

"Yeah, it is," he mumbled.

It seemed almost cheesy that he had brought me to this place. It was almost like a scene out of Twilight or something. I looked around some more before asking "Why did you bring me here?"

"What do you mean?" he asked.

"Is this where you bring all the girls you chase?" I asked, trying not to let him hear my voice crack.

"Vi, what are you talking about?"

"Erin told me you like me," I admitted. "So I was just trying to figure out if this is where you bring all the girls you like when you bring them camping with you."

"For one thing, Vi, besides you, Anna is the only girl I've ever brought camping with me and I wouldn't waste a spot like this on her," he said. "For another, I didn't even know this place existed until we got here."

Something in his voice made me sure that he was being totally sincere. I felt bad for even questioning it. "I'm sorry," I whispered.

He shrugged. "Don't worry about it," he said.

After a few minutes of awkward silence, he moved closer to me. "Violet," he said quietly.

I didn't move away, but I didn't respond. I just continued staring into the sunset.

"Vi," he said again.

I suppressed a sigh. "Yes?"

"Do you think this would be a suitable place for a first kiss?" he asked nervously.

I was taken aback. It took me a moment to gather my thoughts enough to articulate a response. "Well if you're suggesting that we kiss, it wouldn't be our first kiss," I pointed out quietly. "And either way, I've shown no indication of wanting you to kiss me."

I couldn't tell if he was more embarrassed that he had forgotten our first kiss or that I called him out on not making sure I wanted to kiss him first.

"You remember that?" He asked, looking down at the ground.

I shrugged. "Well it was my first kiss," I pointed out. "But I did almost forget... Until I had a dream about it the other night."

"Really?" he asked, looking back up to me.

"Yeah," I admitted, sitting down in the field of clover.

He sat down next to me and put his arms over his knees. "I didn't think it made a lasting impression," he said. "We never talked about it or anything.

I laughed. "We were nine. We didn't know we were supposed to talk about it," I reminded him.

He shrugged. "You know it was my first kiss too," he said.

"Of course I know that! We were nine," I said, laughing. I was surprised by how at ease I felt sitting there with Carter. It was almost as if we had never stopped being friends.

We sat there for a while and continued to watch the sunset. We talked about nothing in particular and laughed a lot until we noticed the sun was sinking below the horizon. Overall, it was actually rather enjoyable.

"We should probably go back," Carter said after a little while. "It's going to get dark soon."

And then we slept on the ground because that's a normal thing that normal people do.

Carter and I left the clearing and went back toward camp. Or at least we thought we were headed back to camp. After fifteen minutes of winding through trails that we thought we had come on, we stopped and looked around. Nothing looked familiar and I wasn't even sure if that was just because it was almost dark.

"Are we lost?" I asked.

"Of course not," Carter said, treading past me down the trail.

I followed for a few more feet before stopping again. "Seriously Carter, we're lost," I told him. "It didn't take us that long to get there."

"Vi, we're okay, I promise," he said, continuing along the trail.

I followed for fifteen more minutes. "Carter, I swear to god," I said. "We are lost."

Carter stopped walking. "Yeah, we are," he said.

I sat down on a log, and ran my hands up and down my bare legs, which were starting to get cold. "What are we going to do?" I asked.

"Sit here and wait for the bears, I guess," he said.

"Wait. There are bears here?!" I asked, unable to hide the terror in my voice.

Carter laughed. "No, Vi. There aren't any bears here," he said.

I rolled my eyes even though I knew he wouldn't be able to see it in the dark. It's an automatic response, okay? "Well then what are we really going to do?" I asked.

"All trails lead to somewhere, right?" he asked with a snicker.

"I'm sure you're astounded by your own cleverness," I started angrily. "But right now is not the time for juvenile behavior!"

"Chill, Vi," he said. "We're going to be okay. We just need to follow the trail and we'll end up back at the campgrounds somewhere, okay?"

"Fine," I huffed, standing back up. "Let's go."

We walked down the trail for another fifteen or twenty minutes, but this time Carter was the one who stopped. "Okay, I'm not so sure this plan is working," he said, admitting defeat.

I looked at him for a second debating silently whether or not I should yell at him. I couldn't very well just let him do something like this without confronting him though. "You did this on purpose, didn't you?"

"No, Violet. I didn't," he said, unconvincingly.

"Seriously, Carter. You got us lost on purpose and I know it!"

"What would getting us lost on purpose accomplish?" he asked, staring at me.

"I've seen plenty of movies. You get us lost. You make me think there's no way back. You convince me we need to sleep out here on the ground, we get cold, and you say that the only way to stay warm is to cuddle. After a while you tell me it would be more effective if we took our clothes off. And at that point, I'm freezing enough to listen; we take our clothes off and..." I explained, irrationally.

"...And?" he asked, gesturing for me to continue.

"Well you know," I said. "A one-thing-leads-to-another sort of thing."

Now it was Carter's turn to roll his eyes. "Is that really how you see me?" he asked.

"No," I sighed.

"You need to start trusting people a little more."

"I've been given a really good reason not to trust one person in particular," I said starkly.

"I can't imagine why," he said sarcastically.

"Well we need a new plan then," I conceded.

We sat down on another log. As I racked my brain for ideas, I started picking up rocks and throwing them across the trail.

"Stop," Carter told me, putting his hand on my arm to prevent me from throwing the next rock. Once the sound of rocks hitting the ground ceased, I heard a familiar peel of laughter.

"Was that Willow?" Carter asked.

"I think it was," I said.

We stood up and followed the trail down just a few more yards and emerged right back in our own campsite. I slapped Carter teasingly across the chest. "Thanks for finding camp," I said with a chuckle. I looked over at Willow who was looking pretty cozy with Liam's arm around her. I raised an eyebrow at her and she gave me a thumbs up, which I took to mean that she was okay with it. I walked over to the table and sat down next to them.

Carter pulled a Gatorade out of the cooler and offered it to me. I took it, and took a long drink.

"How was the hike?" Tyler asked with a snicker. "You were gone for an awfully long time." He nudged Carter with his elbow.

"It was lovely," Carter said.

All the guys continued to snicker. I raised an eyebrow. "Ass butt got us lost," I said with a laugh.

"Ass butt?" Carter said.

I shrugged and took another sip of my Gatorade.

"Oh, you got 'lost'?" Jeff said, making finger quotes as he said the word 'lost'. Everyone laughed, aside from Carter and me. I was pretty sure that my cheeks were turning red. It was a good thing that only light left was from the campfire.

"Yeah. We got lost," Carter said. "In the most literal sense of the word."

"Where's the fun in that?" Liam asked.

Willow slapped Liam playfully on the knee. "Be nice," she quipped.

I stared at the pair for a moment or two. I was bewildered by the progression of this relationship in the last two hours. Before this camping trip Willow barely even acknowledged Liam's existence. Now if I didn't know better I'd think the two of them had been dating for months.

Willow gave me a weird look that reminded me that I was staring at them and I looked away. I realized how cold it was, and for a split second I wished that someone had their arms around me. I quickly remembered that if anyone did, it would be Carter and I was, although irrationally, somewhat irritated with him.

"So the hike was good then," Erin asked, looking at me knowingly.

"It was fine," Carter and I said in unison, exchanging quick smiles.

We all spent a few more hours sitting around the fire laughing and talking. One by one people started moving from the fire to their tents.

"Vi, can we talk?" Willow asked when it was just her, me, Tyler, Erin and Liam left by the fire.

"Sure," I said, standing up. We walked a few feet from the fire.

"Would you mind if I went and slept in Liam's tent?" she asked quietly.

I raised an eyebrow. "Aren't Liam and Carter sharing a tent?"

"Yeah, but it's not like we're going to *do* anything," she said, looking at me like I was crazy for even thinking such a thing.

I shrugged. "Go ahead," I said.

"Are you sure it's okay?" she asked. "I don't want you to be alone on your first night camping.

"I'm fine," I assured her. "Don't worry about it."

I went to my tent and climbed in alone. I put on my pajamas and crawled into my sleeping bag. "It's fine," I reminded myself. "Carter already told me there aren't any bears here."

I laid there for what seemed like hours without a hint of sleep. I was terrified, to say the least. There may not have been bears in this forest but that didn't mean there weren't cougars, bobcats or deer. Could deer even hurt people? I'm sure they could if they wanted to.

After a few minutes of listing wild animals that may or may not have been residing in the very forest that I was supposed to be sleeping in there was a tapping on the side of my tent.

I pulled my sleeping bag over my head and held it tight. It was only a matter of seconds before whatever animal was out there scratched through the thin nylon tent and attacked me.

"Vi," came a whisper through the tent. "Are you awake?" I couldn't tell if Carter was being quiet because he didn't want to wake me up or because he didn't want anyone else to know that he was coming to my tent in the middle of the night.

"Yeah," I whispered back. Feigning sleep would have worked but I was so scared that I was desperate for company. Anyone's company.

"Can I come in?" he asked.

"Yes," I said, sitting up and holding my sleeping bag tightly around myself.

Carter unzipped the tent door and climbed through, zipping it shut behind him. He turned to face me, pausing before crawling closer to me. "Are you okay?" he asked, mild shock apparent in his voice. "You look like you've seen a ghost."

I pulled my sleeping bag even tighter, hoping it would hold in my embarrassment. "I'm scared," I admitted after an impregnated pause.

Carter scooted closer to me so we were sitting right next to each other. "There's nothing to be scared of," he said, obviously trying to hide amusement in his voice.

"It's not funny!" I told him. "I've never been camping before! How do I know there aren't wolves or mountain lions out there?"

This time Carter couldn't suppress his laughter. "Violet, we are at a state park camp ground. They wouldn't let people camp here if it was dangerous."

"Oh," I said, embarrassed.

"You're going to be fine," he assured me. "And besides that, do you think I would let anything happen to you?"

"I highly doubt that if I was being attacked by a rabid raccoon there would be anything you can do to stop it," I told him.

"I could kick it," he said.

I laughed.

"You know, Vi, I had a really good time on our hike tonight," he said. "I'm sorry, though, if you got the wrong idea."

I shrugged. "Don't take it personally," I said. "I just don't have a lot of faith in humanity in general. Though, you haven't been helping that case lately."

"I know I've been bothering you a lot lately," he said. "I just don't think you really understand how I feel."

"Make me understand," I told him.

"Remember how you felt when we stopped being friends?" he asked.

Of course I did. Though I'm not sure he knew how I felt about anything, really. "Yeah," I told him. "I felt like absolute shit. Like I wasn't worth anything at all."

"Yeah," Carter told me. "That's how I felt too. I just felt it four years too late."

"Why, though?"

"Well, I think from a psychological standpoint, that you felt that way at first because it seemed like I didn't care," he started.

"You didn't," I pointed out.

"Not at first," he said. "I was too worried about what the 'popular girls' thought of me."

I snorted. "Typical."

"Well anyway," he continued, ignoring my reaction. "I didn't notice how bad I felt about it until I realized that you didn't care. When I was dating Anna it was so mind numbing that I started to miss being friends with you. Even when we were kids you were always so witty. That's why I showed up at your house that night. I decided that I couldn't stand not being friends with you any longer and had to make it right at that moment."

"Hence showing up at my house at 3 AM," I stated to show him that I understood what he was saying.

"Then when you were unresponsive, and made it clear that you didn't want to be friends with me, that was when I started feeling like shit," he told me. "And I guess I was just a little too persistent, because you don't really want to be friends with me. So maybe I should give up."

"Don't do that," I advised him. I wasn't sure if I should tell him that everything I was doing was Trudi's idea, so I decided that I would talk my way around it. "I haven't really been all that fair to you," I told him.

"So you aren't opposed to being friends with me?" he asked, a confused tone in his voice.

"Well, no," I said, unsure of whether or not I should just explain myself. Fortunately for me he didn't really give me an option.

"Would you care to elaborate?" he asked.

I let out a long sigh. "I was devastated when you stopped being friends with me," I told him.

"I know," he said sadly.

"And then I got over it," I said. "But then you decided you wanted to be friends with me again, and I wasn't sure how I felt about it."

"Why not?" he asked.

"Well, I didn't want to *not* be friends with you," I started. "But I didn't want you to think that I cared so much that I would just go back to giving in without a fight, you know."

"So that's why you were being so difficult? You wanted me to earn it?"

"Well, yeah," I admitted quietly. "I think I went a little too far."

I felt Carter shrug. "Do you think I've earned it yet?"

"I don't know," I said sarcastically, nudging him in the ribs with my elbow.

He laughed and shivered at the same time.

"You don't have to stay here with me," I assured him. "I'm fine."

He snorted. "I don't want to go back to that tent..." he said sounding highly suspicious.

"Umm, may I ask why?" I asked.

"Well, obviously Willow isn't in here," he pointed out, dumbly.

"I see that," I said. "She told me she was going to sleep in your tent."

"Exactly," was all he said.

"Would you care to elaborate now?" I asked.

"I just think that if I wanted to spend the night listening to people making out I would have stayed home and watched 'Skins'."

I could tell that my eyes had widened to the size of dinner plates. "Wait... What?" I asked, completely perplexed. "She said that they wouldn't be doing anything that would make you uncomfortable."

"Yeah, I don't think they realized how loud they were being," he said with a laugh. "But if you want me to leave I can go get into Jeff and Steven's tent."

"No, it's fine," I said. "You can stay." I didn't know which would be more uncomfortable; the two of us sharing a tent or making him squeeze into a tent with two other guys. The latter would probably be more problematic.

"Are you sure?" he asked. "If you're uncomfortable I can go."

"No, it's fine," I promised. "Willow's sleeping bag is still right there if you want to use it."

Carter pulled Willow's sleeping bag next to mine and slipped into it. "Thanks, Vi," he said quietly.

"You're welcome," I mumbled, sliding down in my sleeping bag and resuming my laying position.

After a few minutes, Carter broke the silence by whispering "Vi?"

"Yeah?"

"I missed you," he answered.

"I missed you too," I mumbled sleepily.

"I keep thinking..." Carter said without finishing the thought.

"Keep thinking what?" I pressed.

"Well... What it would have been like if I hadn't listed to Anna," he said. "Do you think I would have ended up with her?"

I rolled over to face him. "Do I look like a crystal ball?" I asked him facetiously.

He laughed. "No, but you know, I'm not sure that she and I would have been endgame either way, you know? I should have seen that before I agreed to date her."

"What do you mean, 'agreed'?" I asked, propping myself up on my arm.

"She'd been begging me to ask her out since we started high school," he admitted. "I never really wanted to, but she wouldn't stop bothering me. This year she just kept telling me that we should go to prom together and that it would be better if we dated before prom, so I finally said I would go out with her so she would stop asking me, and then at least that way I would have a date to prom."

"That doesn't even make sense," I told him. "If her begging you to go out with her was so annoying, what would possibly make you think that she would be less annoying once you agreed?"

Carter groaned. "Don't remind me how idiotic I am…"

"Well as long as you know…" I said.

I laid back down. After a few minutes of silence I shivered loudly. I heard Carter rustle, but I didn't know if he was awake. Seconds later I felt him move closer to me.

"Are you cold?" he asked quietly.

"Yeah," I muttered, leaning into him slightly.

After that Carter fell asleep and his rhythmic breathing soothed me enough that I, too, could fall asleep.

Is the word "platonic" even in people's vocabularies anymore?

The next morning I awoke to movement outside in the campsite. I heard Erin's voice and I knew that the others must be waking up. I opened my eyes and noticed how close Carter was to me. I shut my eyes again, wondering how this was going to be perceived by our friends. I didn't want to wake him up, so I just laid there until he woke up on his own.

"Good morning," he mumbled, his voice hoarse with sleepiness.

"Morning," I reciprocated. "I think everyone else is up."

He sat up and rubbed his eyes. His light brown hair was a mess. He dropped his arms and looked at me. I'm sure I looked like a mess and should probably make a mad dash for the bathroom and clean up before anyone else saw me. Carter, however, smiled when he saw me.

"Thanks for talking last night," he said.

"You're welcome," I said quietly.

"So did we agree that we can be friends again?" he asked.

"Yes."

He nodded and then sighed. "We should probably face the sunshine," he said, wiggling out of the sleeping bag and reaching for the zipper on the door. He unzipped the half-circle tent door and a rush of fresh air came in, cooling us.

Carter crawled through the door and I followed behind him. I stood up straight after crawling through the tent door and zipped it closed so nothing could get in.

"Whoa," Tyler said, seeing Carter and I appear together out of the tent. The guys were all sitting at the picnic table. I assumed Willow and Erin were at the bathroom. I grabbed my bag and headed to the bathroom myself, not wanting to listen to the guys accuse Carter and me of doing something we didn't.

I pushed through the door to the girls' room and set my bag on the counter. I pulled out my towel and walked to the shower area where a few showers were already running. I found an empty one and turned on the water, not saying anything in case it wasn't Willow and Erin that were in there.

After I finished showering I got dressed and went back into the main part of the bathroom. Erin was sitting on the counter while Willow brushed her teeth next to her.

"There she is," Erin said with a smile as I approached. "How was your night?" she asked, not even trying for discretion.

"It was fine," I answered simply, knowing she was assuming something had happened as well. "Probably not as good as Willow's," I added.

Willow glared at me in the mirror for a second before spitting out a mouthful of toothpaste. "You don't know what you're talking about," she said.

"That's not what Liam's tent mate told me when he was forced to sleep in my tent with me," I told her with a chuckle.

"No one forced him out," she said pointedly.

"He told me that sharing a tent with the two of you wouldn't have been any different than staying home and watching 'Skins'," I told her.

Erin snorted and Willow laughed.

"So you talked then, at least?" Erin asked.

"Well it's not like we've had a shortage of alone time in the past twenty-four hours," I reminded them. "Since no one wanted to join us on our little hike yesterday." I eyed both of them suspiciously.

"You know me, I don't like hiking," Willow said.

"I was going to go, I swear," Erin said. "But Tyler said that Carter wanted to talk to you and that I needed to stay."

I rolled my eyes. "Carter didn't need that hike to talk to me," I told them. "Everything he needed to say could have been said any of the number of times he'd tried to talk to me up until this camping trip. I don't know why he couldn't have said it then."

"Give him a break, Vi," Willow said, obviously annoyed. I knew it probably wasn't easy for her, watching me struggle to be friends with my former best friend whom she had replaced.

I peered at myself in the mirror; a sad look had come across my face. "You're right," I conceded.

"Of course I am," Willow said, furrowing her brow, as if she couldn't believe that I was even questioning whether or not she had been right.

I laughed uneasily as I pulled my brush through my long hair. After that, I began to put on my makeup, which wasn't necessarily usual. Erin and Willow sat in the bathroom patiently waiting for me. Every once in a while the two of them would exchange looks and begin to laugh, which made me feel left out or the butt of some inside joke.

After a while I was beginning to get fed up. "What's so funny?" I asked them, not trying to hide my annoyance.

"Nothing," Erin said quickly with another laugh.

Willow sighed. She knew that hiding it from me wouldn't be helpful at all. "We were just wondering when you were going to admit that you like Carter," she admitted.

"Never, because I don't," I told them.

They both laughed more loudly than I thought was necessary. "What?" I demanded.

"Vi, I know you," Willow said. "You just slept on the ground, and you're in the middle of the forest. If you didn't like someone here you wouldn't be putting mascara on right now."

I glared at her through the mirror. "I just don't want to look like a mess," I said.

"Violet," Willow said. It was rare that she called me by my full first name, so I knew she was serious. "You rarely wear mascara to school, and now you want me to believe you care about your appearance in the middle of the woods?"

Erin chuckled.

I grabbed my stuff off the counter and shoved it into my bag. "Why does it matter?" I asked angrily.

"Relax, Vi," Erin said calmly. "We just want to know."

I sighed deeply. They weren't going to believe me if I told them I didn't like Carter. I could lie, and say that I did, but then they'd get the wrong idea about him and I sharing a tent. "We're friends," I stated firmly.

"Well that's progress," Willow said.

I rolled my eyes. "And that's all."

Willow smirked at me. "Uh huh."

I grabbed my bag off of the counter and stormed out of the bathroom, tired of dealing with the abuse they were putting me through.

I walked back to camp, threw my bag into my car and began packing up everything else.

"Is everything okay?" Carter asked from behind me.

"Yeah," I grunted as I struggled to take the tent apart.

He stepped up and began to pull the poles from their sleeves before folding the tent properly. "What's wrong?" he asked.

I shoved sleeping bags into their bags. "I just thought I would be harassed more if I stayed out here with the guys than if I went into the bathroom with the girls, but I guess I was wrong," I told him, breathing heavily.

"What happened?" he asked, concerned.

"Apparently we can't be friends without there being more to it," I told him, as if that made any sense.

"Oh," was all he said.

We continued packing up camp and my car was loaded before Willow and Erin had even made it back from the bathroom. I was sure they were plotting some devious plan to get Carter and me together, but it wasn't going to work. Carter and I had just been able to amend our friendship; there was no way a relationship could come out of this.

I got into my car, intent on leaving Willow behind, but Liam made sure to let her know that we were leaving before I was able to get away.

I was silent for the entire ride home. I knew Carter could tell how upset I was because he didn't try to make jokes or hold conversation with anyone either. I also knew that Willow knew I was pissed. She didn't try saying anything to me the whole way home.

I opted to drop Willow off first, because I didn't want the awkward silence that would ensue if I dropped her off last. I pulled up in front of her house, popped the trunk and waited in the car while Carter and Liam helped her get her stuff out and take it to the house. When Carter and Liam came back to the car, Willow followed.

"Bye, Vi," she said, after hugging Liam goodbye.

"Yeah," I said, pulling back into the street.

I took the guys back to Carter's house, again taking the long way around so my parents wouldn't see me stopping at Carter's house. They got out and pulled their stuff out of the trunk. Liam walked up the steps of the porch, but Carter paused.

He leaned through the passenger side window. "Goodbye, Violet," he said with a grin.

"Goodbye, Carter," I said, putting my car in gear and pulling out of his driveway, only to pull into mine two houses down.

Seriously. You're an adult. Grab a dictionary. Look it up.

I walked into the house through the kitchen, where my mom was standing, peeling a potato.

"How was your camping trip, honey?" she asked me when I walked in.

"Fine," I mumbled. I couldn't go into details with her, even if I wanted to (which, trust me, I didn't.) because she thought I was just with Willow's family.

"Did you say thank you to Mr. and Mrs. Phan?" she asked.

"Yeah, yeah," I said as I walked past her. "Uhm, Mom, I kind of promised Trudi I would have dinner at her house tonight, if that's okay."

"Oh, okay," she said, sounding slightly disappointed. "Have fun then."

I put my bag in my room and left for Trudi's house.

When I walked into Trudi's tiny apartment, she was standing in the kitchen cooking spaghetti.

"Oh, hello," she said when she saw me.

"Hi," I said, unenthusiastically.

A look of realization washed across her face. "How was your camping trip?!" she asked.

I rolled my eyes. "It was okay," I said, noncommittally.

She stared at me for a long time. "Did anything happen?" she finally asked.

"That depends on what your definition of 'anything' is," I told her.

This time she rolled her eyes at me. "Spill the beans," she demanded, stirring the pot of spaghetti sauce.

I sighed. "Everything was going just fine, and then Carter wanted to go for a hike, and no one else wanted to go with him, so I went. We ended up in a meadow at sunset and he asked if it would be a suitable place for a first kiss-"

"YOU KISSED?!" she interrupted.

"No... I pointed out that it wouldn't be our first kiss and he dropped it."

"You should have kissed him," she said.

"Whatever. Anyway, we decided to go to the campsite, but got lost and-"

"So you stopped in the woods and kissed?" she interrupted again. She put a pot of water on the stove to boil spaghetti noodles in.

"Trudi, let me just say this now. We. Did. Not. Kiss. At all," I told her. "Can I finish now?"

"I don't really know if I want to hear it now," she said, turning her nose up in the air.

"Okay, I'll just leave then," I threatened.

"Fine, finish," she said unenthusiastically.

"So we finally found camp and everything was fine again, except Willow and Carter's friend Liam were all cuddly and stuff. So anyway, everyone was going to bed and Willow told me that she was going to sleep in Carter and Liam's tent," I explained. "But that everything would be fine because they weren't going to do anything that would make Carter uncomfortable," I added for good measure.

"Okay, so everything was fine then?" she asked, raising an eyebrow.

"Well yeah, but that's not everything. So I was really scared, because, you know, I was sleeping in the forest, which is something I've never done before, and I didn't know what kind of animals there were out there. Then I heard a tapping on the side of the tent and all but peed my pants," I explained.

"There were animals in your campsite?!" Trudi asked, apparently appalled. She had never been camping either and I guess she didn't really understand what I was trying to say.

"No, Carter was outside my tent," I said plainly. "He asked if he could come in, and since I was so scared, I said yes."

Trudi's eyes were huge and she looked like she was on the verge of tears. "Oh my gosh, Trudi," I said. "NOTHING HAPPENED!"

She sniffed and rubbed her eyes. "Of course it didn't," she said. "I didn't think that anything happened!"

I rolled my eyes again. "Right. Anyway, we talked for a little while and agreed that we could really, actually be friends, and we fell asleep. But we were the last to wake up in the morning, so everyone saw us leave the tent together and assumed something happened. Willow and Erin kind of harassed me about it," I said. I could feel my sinuses burning.

"What happened?" she asked, genuinely curious by this point.

"They didn't believe me when I told them nothing happened, and Willow kept badgering me about when I was going to tell her that I liked Carter. Then when I told her I don't like Carter she yelled at me. Then her and Erin kept laughing at me for putting on makeup, so I left the bathroom and packed my stuff up. I was just going to leave and not take Willow with me, but Liam went and got her before I had the chance to drive away."

That's probably a good thing," Trudi pointed out. "If you had left Willow there it would have caused serious problems for your friendship."

"Our friendship already has serious problems," I told her.

She pulled the pot of noodles over to the sink and drained them, setting the strainer back in the empty pot. "Do you think that's going to last long?" she asked me.

"Carter and I weren't friends for four years," I reminded her.

She rolled her eyes at me again, as she began dishing us both plates of spaghetti. "Did you really just compare your friendship with Willow to your friendship with Carter?" she asked me.

"Yeah, I did. They're the only two important friendships I've ever had," I pointed out.

She sighed in defeat. "I guess you have a point," she said.

"Of course I have a point."

She handed me my plate of spaghetti and I started twirling the noodles with my fork absently.

"Maybe you should just admit that you like Carter," she said between bites of spaghetti.

I dropped my fork on my plate and groaned. "I would admit that I like Carter if, and only if I liked Carter!"

Trudi snorted.

"You're acting like Willow," I told her angrily.

"Vi, that's because Willow and I know you."

"Obviously not well enough. If I liked Carter I wouldn't be ashamed of it," I told her.

"You would if you were trying to prove something," she told me.

I sat in silence, not wanting to have to explain myself to my own aunt. I couldn't believe that she and Willow didn't believe that I wouldn't admit to them that I liked Carter. I mean, sure, at one point in my life I may have had slight feelings for him, but it had taken me this long to even consider being friends with him. I don't see how they could honestly think that I liked him now.

"But... You can't admit it to anyone else until you admit it to yourself, honey," Trudi said, standing up and taking her plate to the sink.

I ate a few bites of spaghetti and made my way to the sink. "And if that ever happens, you'll be the first to know," I assured her.

I helped my aunt with the dishes and told her I needed to go home.

Once I got back to my car, I turned the radio up as loud as I could stand it to hopefully drown out my thoughts. However, a Taylor Swift song came on and made even me question my emotions. Was I lying, not only to everyone else, but to myself as well? If I was lying to myself, wouldn't I know?

If I was, I just wasn't admitting it to myself because that would be too easy. Carter and I were just now able to be friends, and I still couldn't understand how anyone thought a relationship was going to come out of it. No matter how many times I thought about it, I still couldn't wrap my mind around it.

I pulled into my driveway a little bit after nine. The lights were off downstairs, so I knew I had to be quiet coming in. I slipped through the back door and tip-toed up the stairs to my room.

"Violet?" came my father's voice.

"Yeah?" I whispered.

"You need to stop taking advantage of your aunt just because you don't want to be here," he told me before disappearing behind his closed bedroom door.

I rolled my eyes. Of course I didn't want to be here. I was the forgotten child, lost when they decided to try for their perfect nuclear family. My aunt was the only one who really wanted me around all the time.

I stepped into my room and shut the door loudly, not caring about upsetting my parents. I grabbed my backpack and pulled out my books to check over my homework and make sure it was all done. After that, I went to bed.

The next morning I walked into the cafeteria and saw Willow sitting with Liam at our usual table. I debated whether or not I should go sit with them when Carter came and stood next to me.

"Are you going to sit down?" he asked.

"I don't really know if I want to talk to Willow," I told him.

"What did she do?" he asked.

"What?" I looked up at him and saw he was looking at me with a concerned expression. "Oh, she was just being an asshole yesterday when she saw us coming out of the tent together."

"So she didn't believe you when you said nothing happened between us?"

"Not exactly," I said, not sure how I wanted to approach this subject with Carter.

"Well then what?"

"She believed me when I said that nothing happened, but she didn't exactly... believe that I didn't want something to happen."

He stared at me in disbelief. "That doesn't make sense," he said finally.

"She asked when I was going to tell her that I like you," I clarified. "And then when I told her that I didn't like you and that we were just friends she laughed in my face and called me a liar."

Carter rolled his eyes. "Well I know how much you hate letting other people win, so let's go," he said, grabbing my arm and leading me toward the table. He sat down and gently pulled me down in the chair next to him.

Willow raised an eyebrow, but I chose to ignore her. Instead, I pretended to find the ring I was wearing so interesting that I could hardly feign attention for anything else. I twisted it around my finger and listened to Carter and Liam talk about the camping trip. Willow chimed in a few times. I remained silent until Liam addressed me directly.

"Did you have fun, Violet?" he asked.

"I guess for the most part," I said, shooting a quick glare at Willow.

Willow stared at me in what seemed like disbelief, but I knew she wasn't oblivious to how I felt. I stared back as if to challenge her to ask me what I meant.

"Are you serious right now?" she asked, angrily.

"Uh, yeah, I am," I said simply.

"So you're mad at me for *pointing out the obvious*?" she asked.

"You weren't pointing out the obvious," I told her. "You were accusing me of something that wasn't true."

"Hey now," interjected Liam. "Calm down."

I turned my glare toward him. "Then tell your girlfriend to stop being a hypocrite," I told him.

He turned around and looked at her. She stared at me angrily. "How am *I* the hypocrite in this situation?"

"Let's see, you through a fit because I wouldn't tell you that I like Carter, when I don't, but you never even told me that you like Liam." I pointed out, giving Carter an apologetic look for announcing that I don't like him.

"That's because I didn't know that I liked Liam until it happened," she said.

"Well then why can't you just accept the fact that Carter and I are just friends?" I asked. "Why do you think that I wouldn't tell you if I liked him?"

She sighed in defeat. "Okay, fine. I guess if you did like him you would probably tell me."

"You would be the first to know," I agreed.

"What if I want to be the first to know?" Carter asked with a smirk.

I furrowed my brow. "You would know shortly after, I guess," I told him with a shrug.

He laughed and I smiled back to him, thankful that he dragged me over here, and inevitably caused Willow and me to resolve our issues. I opened my mouth to thank him just as the bell rang. I grabbed my bag, making sure I had my keys, and left for class without thanking him at all.

When I got to class I pulled out my phone and texted Carter "Thank you."

"You're welcome," came his response a few minutes later.

The rest of the day went by uneventfully as usual, although the last few weeks hadn't been typical. Lunch was quiet because I still felt uneasy around Willow and it didn't help that Liam was on her like white on rice whenever they had a chance to be together. Thankfully Carter sat with us again which eased the tension. I never thought once in the past four years that I would be thankful for Carter's presence but I really was.

***

In order to avoid spending time with my family without 'using' my aunt, I made it to work twenty minutes early and decided to walk around the mall. As I was walking past Pac Sun I saw Anna with her friend Leah.

"Yeah, so they went on their camping trip that I always used to go on with them, and I wasn't even invited," Anna said.

"Well you *did* break up with him," Leah told her.

"Yeah, but that doesn't mean I don't want him to try to get me back," she pointed out. "But that's not the point. He invited *Violet Montgomery*," Anna said my name with a whisper. I knew she couldn't see me because their backs were turned to me as they sorted through bracelets at one stand, while I looked at phone cases on the opposite stand, our backs toward each other.

"Ew, why?" Leah asked.

"I have no idea," Anna said. She sounded like she was on the verge of tears. "And Jeff said that Carter slept in her tent."

"You don't think…?" Leah didn't finish her thought.

"I don't want to," Anna said. "But it would make sense. I mean, he had been sneaking over to her house in the middle of the night. They were probably doing it the whole time, before we even broke up."

My eyes widened and I felt the color rush to my cheeks. I tried to remain calm so I could listen to the rest of the conversation.

"Probably," said Leah. "I've always thought there was something weird about that girl. Wasn't she, like, super obsessive of him in middle school?"

"Oh yeah," Anna answered her. "She would follow him around like a puppy dog and cry whenever he talked to anyone else. It was so pathetic. It's obvious that they were doing something, even back then." She said that last bit with a tone of absolute disgust.

I snorted and immediately covered my mouth, worried that they had heard me. None of it was true. I never showed obsessive tendencies toward anyone, not even Carter.

"He probably just feels sorry for her," Leah tried reassuring Anna.

"There's no doubt about that," Anna agreed. "He couldn't possibly like a girl like her. I mean, he's hot. He's just getting a free boink out of it."

I rolled my eyes. No one was getting anything out of it. I decided I had had enough eavesdropping on this conversation, so I turned around and walked right past them, back to the food court. I didn't even care if they saw me.

I arrived at work three minutes late and the only one there was Willow. She stared me down for a second, and I was sure she was going to angrily point out that I was late, but one look at me told her something wasn't right.

"What's wrong?" she asked.

"I just heard Tweedle-Dumb and Tweedle-Dumber having a conversation about me," I told her.

"What were they saying?" she asked, knowing exactly who I was talking about.

"Well," I said with a sigh, not sure where to begin. Basically they concluded that Carter and I have been having sex since we reached puberty, and of course, being the assholes that we are, we didn't stop while he was dating Anna."

"Wait, what?" Willow asked, confusion on her face.

"Anna told Leah that Carter only invited me on the camping trip to have sex with me, and when Leah asked if she was sure, Anna told her that he snuck over to my house in the middle of the night, and we've probably been having sex forever, and that Carter only sees me as a free 'boink'."

Willow rolled her eyes. "If Carter saw you as a free boink don't you think he would have, you know, tried to boink you by now?"

"I know, I didn't say I believed her," I told her. "I just don't want this rumor going around school and making us look bad."

I was really annoyed. I could understand why Anna would feel the need to start a rumor about me, but didn't she think that she had done enough damage in the past four years? I grabbed my phone and sent another text to Carter. "We need to talk. Can you come to the mall right now?"

Shortly after I sent the message, Anna and Leah came and sat down near the Orange Julius booth. I rolled my eyes.

About fifteen minutes later, Carter showed up and walked straight up to the counter. Anna noticed him and watched him walk up to me.

"What's up?" he asked.

I nodded my head toward Anna and Leah. "The rumor mill has been working overtime this week," I said. "And it's only Monday."

"Wait, what are they saying?" he asked, shooting a dirty look at their table, which went unnoticed.

"Apparently the only reason you invited me camping is so you could get a 'free boink' out of it," I informed him.

"Is that so?" he asked with a roll of his eyes.

"Oh, yeah," I said. "But I haven't gotten to the best part yet."

"Do continue," he said.

"Well that wasn't even our first time," I told him. "Apparently we've been doing it for years. And when you came to my house at 3 AM two weeks ago, it was to have sex. Oh, and you've been sneaking away to my house multiple times a week to have sex with me, especially while you were dating Anna."

"Was I any good?" Carter asked, raising an eyebrow.

Leave it to Carter to make jokes. "Carter, this isn't funny!"

"For someone who doesn't care what people think, you sure care a lot about what people think," he said.

Willow snorted.

I stared at him in disbelief. "I don't care what people think, to a point," I informed him. "When people think that I've been knockin' boots with someone that I haven't even talked to in almost four years, yeah, that's something I care about."

Carter sighed. "I'll go talk to her," he said. He turned around and walked toward their table, pulling a chair out and sitting down. I watched him for a second and then realized that I should be helping Willow do work stuff.

"Get over it, Anna!" I heard Carter say loudly after about five minutes. I looked toward the table. Carter was standing, his fists clenched, and Anna was grabbing his arm, looking pathetic.

He shook her off and moved back over to my counter where I was finishing up my closing duties. I glanced at him for a moment and then resumed watching Anna storm away from the food court.

"What happened?" Willow asked.

"She begged me to 'dump the weirdo,' meaning you," he said with a nod toward me, "and take her back."

Willow snorted again. "Well I guess starting rumors about Vi is how she got you the last time," she pointed out.

"I told her to leave me alone and get over it," he told us.

"That much we heard," I told him with a chuckle.

Just then, we heard a sob and looked over to see Anna standing at the edge of the food court looking inconsolable. Leah was sympathetically touching her arm while glaring at me.

"If I didn't know any better, I'd say you broke up with her," Willow said with a laugh. Carter smiled but didn't say anything.

Willow and I finished our work, with Carter looming over our counter. I wasn't sure why he felt the need to stay there, but he did. Anna was still sitting in a chair sobbing at the end of the food court (what a drama queen!), which led me to believe that he didn't want to walk past her alone.

We closed the gate at 9 pm on the dot, and walked out of the food court. As we walked past Anna and Leah, Carter slipped his arm around my waist and pulled me closer to him. I didn't protest, only because I knew what he was trying to do. Anna let out another wail and Leah glared at us.

As we got out of eyeshot of the food court, Carter retracted his arm. "Sorry about that," he said quietly.

"It's fine," I said, elbowing him in the ribs playfully. "I always knew you couldn't resist the smell of hotdogs."

Carter walked Willow and me to the parking lot. I unlocked my car and opened the door.

"I'll see you later?" Carter said hopefully.

"Yeah," I agreed. "Tomorrow." I had to specify before he showed up at my house in the middle of the night again.

Carter smiled and turned to walk to his car. As I sat down in my driver's seat, Willow wrenched open my passenger door and climbed in.

"What was *that* about?" she asked.

"You were there," I reminded her.

"Yeah, but I didn't remember the agreement that you were going to walk through the mall like a couple."

"We weren't walking like a couple," I told her. "He just wants to torture Anna, which she deserves."

"I can't deny that," Willow said. "But if he *really* wanted to torture her, he should have kissed you."

"Why does everyone keep saying that we should kiss?" I asked, annoyed.

"Because you should," she said simply.

"We're friends," I reminded her. "Just friends."

"And Rome is just a city," she said.

I raised an eyebrow. "What are you talking about?"

Willow stared at me like I was an idiot, which was probably because she was thinking that I was an idiot. "You and Carter are just friends like Bill Clinton and Monica Lewinsky were just coworkers."

"So you're saying that Carter and I are having an extramarital affair while one of us is the president and the other is a White House intern?"

She rolled her eyes. "You know what I mean, Violet."

"There is nothing going on between me and Carter!" I told her. "I don't know how many times I'm going to have to tell you that."

She shrugged. "If you won't admit it to yourself, you can't admit it to me," she said, pushing the door open and getting out of the car. "See you tomorrow."

I drove home, showered and got into bed. Sleep came uneasily once again because I kept thinking about what Willow had said about not being able to admit it to myself. I thought about what I heard Anna saying at the mall, and the camping trip. Then I remembered Willow and Erin had been planning something that they wouldn't tell me about. I wondered what it was.

Did anyone not see this coming?

"It's green," Willow said to Liam as I sat down at our table in the cafeteria the next morning.

"What's green?" I asked.

"Nothing," Willow and Liam said in unison, which made me think that something was going on."

I raised an eyebrow. "It's cool. Don't tell me." I said sarcastically.

"Okay," said Willow, obviously intent on not telling me.

The bell rang and there was still no sign of Carter. *That's strange*, I thought to myself. I shrugged it off, remember that I shouldn't care, and went to class.

Halfway through second period I felt my phone vibrate in my pocket and slipped it out, reading the message under my desk.

"Can we talk at lunch?" Carter had texted. I felt a lurch in my stomach. I had no idea what he could possibly want to talk about.

"Yeah, sure," I texted back.

"Meet me at my locker," he said.

The rest of second period and all of third period seemed to drag on and go by way too fast at the same time. I wasn't sure what he wanted to talk about or even whether it was good or bad. Anticipation was never a feeling I enjoyed either way.

When the bell finally rang for lunch, I waited by Carter's locker for him like he told me to. Anna walked by and saw me standing at his locker, a place I'm sure she waited for him many times. She gave me a dirty look, and I returned it gratefully.

When the hallway started to clear out, I was wondering if Carter had forgotten about me. Just as I decided I was tired of waiting for him, I saw him come down the hall.

"Hey," he said.

"Hello."

"I need to ask you a question, but I'm not sure how to ask it," he said quietly. I could tell that he was slightly nervous.

"What's up?" I asked him.

"Well I was... I was kind of wondering if..." he stammered. "I was wondering if you would go to prom with me?"

I looked at him for a second, struggling internally. Prom wasn't really something I could see myself partaking in, but I didn't want to say no and leave him in a lurch. But if I said yes, I would only have two weeks to find a dress. And then Willow would be all alone, her plans cancelled.

"Just as friends," he added, as I was about to give my answer.

"Well…" I started, unsure of how to let him down easily. "I already kind of had plans with Willow," I told him.

"Oh, yeah," he said sadly. "I just kind of assumed Liam would ask her."

I hadn't thought about Liam, but was sure that if he did ask her, she would have said no, or at least told me she was cancelling our plans, which she hadn't.

"I don't think she really wants to go to prom either," I told Carter with an apologetic look on my face.

His face dropped. "Oh, right," he said. "I forgot." He turned and walked away. I could tell he was embarrassed.

"Carter, wait," I called after him.

He turned around, and I could tell he was trying to gain composure. "Yeah?" he said after a second.

"If Willow and Liam go to prom, I'll go with you," I said. I was annoyed that I was even making this proposition because I really did not want to go to prom, but seeing him like this was making me even more upset than a night of teenage normalcy would.

He half smiled at me. "You don't have to do that," he said, shaking his head.

"You have to know that the reason I don't want to go has nothing to do with you," I pleaded.

"Sure," he said, walking away again.

I sighed in defeat.

After school, I made it out of the school without running into Carter or Willow. I got in my car and drove to Aunt Trudi's apartment. I pushed the door open and found her in her room folding laundry. I flopped myself onto her bed.

"What's wrong?" she asked knowingly.

"I don't even know," I groaned.

"Explain," she demanded.

"Carter asked me to prom," I said, ignoring the resulting squeal. "And I said no."

"Why would you do that?" she asked me, staring me down.

"Because I already have plans for that night, and I didn't want to ditch Willow," I told her. "And could you really see *me* at prom?"

"You could wear my purple dress," she told me, as if trying to bribe me.

"Well he's mad at me now, so he's probably coming up with someone else to take," I told her.

"Come on, he can't be that mad at you."

"He looked pretty mad when he left," I told her.

She stared at me for a few seconds before silently turning back to her laundry. I knew I shouldn't have told her but I needed to talk to someone. Since I would never talk to my mother about something like this and Willow would think I was blaming her for not going to prom, Trudi was my only option.

Trudi had always wanted me to have the regular teenage experience, and to be honest, I just wasn't into it. She had urged me to try out for cheerleading my freshman year and was disappointed when I didn't. She had tried to convince Willow to nominate me for homecoming court sophomore year, but thankfully Willow's was the only anonymous nomination. And now, my junior year, it was prom.

I knew further explanation would just lead to an argument, so I chose to remain silent unless asked. I just lied there, staring up at the ceiling until she said something.

"Call him," she commanded after a few prolonged seconds of silence.

"And say what?" I said, trying to cover up my annoyance with skepticism.

"That you'll go to prom with him," she said.

"But I'm not going to prom with him," I said simply.

"Violet, one of these days you're going to regret not doing anything teenagers are supposed to do!"

"Who says teenagers are *supposed* to go to prom?" I asked, getting up and pacing my aunt's bedroom. "Why is it necessary for all teenagers to participate in archaic traditions that no one even really wants to be a part of? Why should I have to spend hours making myself look better than I take the time to look on any other day to wear an uncomfortable dress and listen to crappy music in a cafeteria full of sweaty people that I don't want to associate with in my day to day life?"

"Cool it, Vi," Trudi said, raising her hands in defeat. "I was just saying that one day you might have a daughter, or a niece, and if you miss this opportunity to go to your prom, you won't be able to convince them to go to their prom."

"Okay, Trudi, you're missing the point," I told her. "I don't feel that it is necessary for me to go to prom. If I have a daughter or a niece who wanted to go to prom, then I would be encouraging enough, but if she didn't want to go to prom, I wouldn't try to force her to!"

"No one's forcing anyone to do anything, Violet!" she shouted at me. "I just don't want you to miss the opportunity!"

"It's not a missed opportunity if it's an opportunity I have absolutely no desire in taking!"

"Fine, don't go," she told me.

"I won't," I said stubbornly.

After that, I left my aunt's apartment and went home. It was only four-thirty, which meant I was going to have to eat dinner with my family. I walked into the house, attempting to draw as little attention to myself as possible. After the incident with my father the other night, I didn't really want to see any of them right now.

I walked up the stairs quietly and shut myself into my room. I'm sure that what Trudi was saying had some validity. I mean, she had been my age once. But I honestly couldn't even picture myself at the prom. But, I guess at least I had a dress option if I did want to go.

I sighed and opened my computer. I scrolled through my Facebook news feed before noticing the green circle next to Carter's name in my chat bar.

"Can we talk?" I messaged him.

"Sure," he said.

"I know you're mad at me, but I really want you to know that it's nothing personal," I said.

"I know, Violet. I'm not mad. I was just disappointed. I thought it would be really fun to go with you."

I groaned to myself, wondering why I had thought it would be a good idea to talk to him in the first place. He was making me feel even worse about my decision to say no to him.

"I don't doubt how fun it would be," I lied. "I just… I don't have time to find a dress, and I'm not much one to care about my appearance…" I couldn't think of any more excuses to include in the list.

"Your appearance is always fine," he assured me.

"Thanks," I said, noncommittally. "I'm really sorry, Carter," I added.

"It's fine. Don't worry about it. It's just junior prom. I still have another year to convince you before it's really too late."

I had no idea what to say to this notion. "Hopefully it won't take much next year," I said, giving into the idea that maybe I would be more willing to go to my senior prom.

"I'll keep working on it," he said.

"You don't have a lot of room for improvement," I told him honestly.

The truth was I would have loved to go to prom with Carter, if I would have loved to go to prom. My defiance obviously stemmed from not wanting to give in to teenage pop-culture stereotypes as opposed to not wanting to go to the prom with Carter.

"Junior prom isn't that important," he repeated. "I don't need to go."

I felt worse and worse as this conversation progressed, so I decided to end it right then and there. "Thanks for being so understanding," I told him. "I have some homework to do, so I'll talk to you tomorrow, okay?"

"Yeah, tomorrow. ☺" he said.

I shut my laptop and stretched in my chair. It was five-fifteen. Dinner would be ready soon. My family liked to eat ridiculously early so that the kids could take baths and go to bed at a reasonable hour. I wondered if I could get away with staying in my room, not making a peep and missing dinner because they hadn't noticed I'd already come home. I decided to try this.

I pulled out my copy of To Kill a Mockingbird and started where I had left off. I read for a bout fifteen minutes before there was a knock on my door.

"Violet, it's time for dinner," my mother said through the closed door.

"Okay," I said, trying my hardest to suppress a groan. "I'm coming."

I walked down the stairs, doing my best to bottle up my annoyance. I took my usual spot at the table and sipped on my water.

"How was your day, Violet?" my father asked gruffly.

"It was fine," I said quietly. Conversations in my family never lasted for more than two lines of dialogue so I wasn't surprised when he immediately turned his attention to Daniel and Liana.

I ate my dinner in silence, and when I was finished, I excused myself from the table. I went back to my room to continue my reading.

Something smells fishy. It's probably just the red herring.

The next two days went by relatively quickly and uneventfully. On Thursday, that changed.

I sat down at my usual spot in the cafeteria that morning. "I'm gonna make cookies for our anti-prom night," I told Willow. "What kind do you want?"

"Actually…" Willow started with a semi-sad expression on her face. "I kind of… agreed to go to prom with Liam."

I stared at her in disbelief for what seemed like twenty minutes, but was, in reality, probably more like four seconds. "Oh," was the only response I could muster.

"I'm really sorry, Vi," she told me. "I didn't really know how to tell you."

"I just wish I would have known sooner…" I trailed off.

"Why?" she asked, an eyebrow raised.

"Carter asked me to go to prom with him, as friends," I added the last part so she wouldn't accuse me of more than what was really there.

"And?"

"And I told him no because I didn't want to flake on you," I informed her.

She looked solemn. "Oh. Can you tell him you changed your mind?" she asked.

"I told him that if, for any reason, you ended up going to prom, I would go with him, but he said I didn't have to. So now I feel bad."

"Why should you feel bad?" she asked.

"He looked really upset when I said no."

"Well yeah. Did you think getting rejected by the person you've loved your whole life would feel good?"

"Oh, shut up, Willow," I said. I knew as well as she did that Carter hadn't loved me his whole life. If he had, we would have never stopped talking.

Willow rolled her eyes at me. "You're just oblivious to it."

"Yeah, okay," I responded, not really wanting to argue about this. I was pretty sure that if Carter had loved me his whole life, I would have noticed at some point. Although I had gotten over the initial shock, it did still seem odd that he wanted to be friends again, so suddenly, but that didn't make me assume that he was in love with me. I felt like if he had been in love with me, the last four years, including his relationship with Anna, wouldn't have happened.

I had to admit (to no one other than myself, of course) that I was still slightly damaged from the events of the past, which may have been blinding me from seeing what was really going on here. But if there was more going on than what I could actually see, I wasn't entirely sure I actually wanted to see it.

As the final bell of the day rang, I walked out of the school into the parking lot. I saw Carter near his car, Anna standing in front of him with a hand on her hip.

"Just tell me why you won't take me to prom!" she demanded, sounding angry.

"I already told you, Anna," he said. "You dumped me so I'm not obligated to take you to the prom."

Anna rolled her eyes and shifted her weight from one foot to the other. "Well I'm still giving you the chance to take me to prom," she said, as if that were some sort of prize.

"Anna, I'm not going to prom at all, much less with you!" he nearly shouted. After he said that, he turned his gaze and saw me standing there. His face lost some sort of its composure upon seeing me. "I have to go now," he said forcefully getting into his car.

Anna stormed away as Carter started his engine. Before he had the chance to move out of his parking space, I opened his passenger side door.

"Can we talk?" I asked.

"Are you going to give me the option?" he retorted.

"Probably not."

"Didn't think so.

"Willow and Liam are going to prom," I said simply.

"I know. I actually knew that before I asked you to go with me…"

"Why didn't you say anything then?" I asked.

"Because you were so set on not going to prom that I didn't want to make you have to come up with another excuse," he said with a shrug.

"Well I told you if they went, I would go with you," I reminded him.

"Don't bother," he said.

"What?"

"Don't bother coming to prom with me out of pity. I'm not going to force you into an evening of teenage normalcy that you wouldn't enjoy," he said, putting it the exact same way I had, which almost made me want to go.

"Look, I know you want to go to prom," I said. "And I feel like since I've been such a bitch for the past few weeks, I probably owe you. Let me go to prom with you."

"Now you sound like Anna, begging me to go to prom with you," he said, smiling.

I snorted. "Do you still think *I'm* the one who was obsessed with you?"

He laughed. "No," he admitted. "But I'm still not going to take you to prom."

"Fine," I said, pushing the door open and getting out of his car. "That's good actually, because I didn't really want to go."

I walked away and got into my car without another word. I honestly didn't want to go to the prom, but for some reason I was still feeling the sting of rejection. I didn't know why I felt this way, so I attributed it to the fact that I'm too stubborn to be okay with someone disagreeing with me.

I drove home and walked into the house. My mom was in the living room, reading a book.

"Violet, can I talk to you?" she said when I walked in.

"I guess," I sighed, dropping my backpack on the floor and sitting down in a chair.

"It's about prom," my mother said, pushing her glasses to the top of her head, holding her place in her book with her finger.

I rolled my eyes and groaned. "Why does everyone think I need to go to prom?" I asked, almost yelling.

"I just don't think you handled it properly, Violet," she said sternly.

"Handled what?" I asked, raising an eyebrow. I didn't like that she knew anything about that.

"The situation with Carter Greenspan," she stated.

"How do you know about that?" I asked her, approaching furious.

"Lisa Greenspan called me," she said, staring me down. I don't know why my mother always found it necessary to use any member of the Greenspan family's last name when speaking of them. I had known these people my whole life.

I rolled my eyes at her again. "Why does it matter?"

My mother put her hand to her forehead, almost as if she was fighting a brain splitting headache. "If you only knew the trouble I went through…" she muttered to herself.

"Excuse me?" I said. "I can hear you." I knew she wasn't going to like my attitude, but I was becoming very annoyed with her.

Her head snapped up and I saw that her eyes were becoming wet. "Nothing that concerns you," she snapped. "Now go to your room."

I got up out of the chair and picked my backpack up off of the floor. "Actually, I'll do better than that. I'll go to Trudi's," I said before turning and walking right back out the front door.

On my drive to Trudi's I called Willow.

"Hello?" she answered her phone.

"My mom just yelled at me for turning Carter down and is being unusually cryptic. I'm kind of worried," I told her.

"What do you mean, cryptic?" she asked.

"When I asked her why it mattered why I turned Carter down she said 'If you only knew what I went through,' and then when I asked what the hell she was talking about she told me it was none of my business," I explained.

"Weird," was all Willow said. I could tell she was eating.

"I'm going to see if Trudi will tell me anything," I informed her. "In case you want to stop by."

"I can't," Willow said. "I have to do some prom shopping. You can tell me what you find out tomorrow at school."

"Okay, bye," I said.

The conversation had lasted just the right amount of time, and I was now pulling into my aunt's parking lot.

I pushed the door open and found my aunt making a sandwich.

"Do you want one?" she asked when I walked in, not even turning to see that it was me. She somehow always knew when I was coming.

"No thanks," I said. "I need to talk to you about something."

"What's up, buttercup?" she asked.

I sat down at the table before saying anything, but then I finally repeated the scene that had happened at my house.

"What do you think it meant?" I asked when I was finished.

"Well you know how competitive she is with the Greenspans," she reminded me.

"Yeah, but it seemed like it was… more than that," I tried to explain.

"Vi, I wouldn't take it as anything more than that," she told me.

It was usually blatantly obvious when Trudi was hiding something from me, but this time I couldn't tell. She seemed sincere when she told me that I shouldn't think too much of it, but something about the way she wasn't overanalyzing it like she usually did with everything else made me suspicious.

"Are you sure?" I asked, hoping I could coax something out of her.

"Positive," was all she said before filling her mouth up with sandwich.

I raised an eyebrow at her and decided not to question it further.

***

The next morning at school, Willow, Liam and I sat in our usual spot in the cafeteria. I was telling Willow about my not-so-helpful conversation with Trudi the night before when Carter sat down with us. I think he felt better about the situation now that he had the chance to reject me.

"What are you talking about?" he asked.

I told him about what had happened at home and the resulting conversation with my aunt. When I was finished, he looked shocked.

"That's so strange," he said after a few seconds.

"Why?" I asked, knowing that there was something more than the obvious going on.

"When I told my mom you had said no to my prom invitation, she said it was too bad, considering. But she wouldn't tell me considering *what*."

"That doesn't make any sense," I said, trying to work things out in my mind. "Did she elaborate?" I asked, not hiding the concern in my voice.

"I asked what she meant and she said 'Things could have been much worse, but now we know that everything is okay,' and just kind of trailed off. Then when I asked what she was talking about she looked like she had forgotten I was there and told me it didn't matter," he said.

I stared at him for a second before looking to Willow. She usually had all the answers but this time even she was stumped. "I don't know, Vi," she said after some silent analyzing. "You're going to have to do some digging."

I contemplated this, but my thoughts were interrupted by Carter.

"Maybe we should go to prom together though, since your mom did so much work, and it could have been much worse."

I turned to look at him, with what must have been an amused look plastered across my face. He was trying so hard to get what he wanted and I really had to commend him for that. Silently, of course.

"I told you I would go to prom with you," I said, watching the look of hope wash over his face. "And then you told me no," I added, gauging his crashing disappointment to be somewhat high.

"Tell ya what," I said, reaching out and putting my hand on his upper arm. I couldn't help but notice how firm his muscles were underneath my hand. "If I can find a dress, I'll go."

I felt bad for even making the proposition, because in all reality there was basically no chance of me finding a dress that I liked.

"Don't Vi," he said. "I'm not going to make you do anything you don't want to do."

I looked at him for a minute, trying to think of a way to make it up to him. "Do you want to help me figure out what our parents are talking about?" I asked.

He shrugged. "I don't think we'll be able to," he said. "They wouldn't tell us when we asked them. Your aunt didn't tell you anything. Our dads aren't going to say anything."

I sighed. He was probably right. There really was no point in trying to figure out something my mother didn't want me to know. She was sneaky.

Carter smiled at me. "Whatever it is though, I'm sure it's not that big of a deal."

The bell rang and the day went by as usual. After school, I was walking out to my car when I felt my phone vibrate in my pocket. It went on long enough to signify a phone call as opposed to a text message. I pulled it out of my pocket and the screen told me that it was Trudi calling me.

"Hello," I answered.

"Hi," she said quietly. "I just got a phone call from my sister telling me that if you come over today I am to send you home immediately. Do you know anything about that?"

I was puzzled. "No," I told her honestly. "Why wouldn't she just tell me to come home after school?" I asked.

"No idea," said Trudi. "Did she know you were coming over yesterday?"

"Yes. I told her that's where I was going when she sent me to my room because I was 'asking too many questions'."

"She's probably worried I'm going to tell you something she doesn't want you to know," Trudi said.

I had no idea what that was supposed to mean. "Do you know something that she doesn't want me to know?"

"I don't even know," Trudi told me, her voice sincere. "Your mom has always been very secretive."

"That doesn't surprise me," I said. "But if you don't know anything then why am I not allowed to see you?"

"I don't know Vi, but we probably shouldn't do anything more to upset her. Obviously, whatever is going on is really bothering her."

"Yeah, you're probably right," I told her.

We finished the conversation, and I headed straight home, since I wasn't allowed to go to Trudi's and had nowhere else to go.

I walked in the door and spotted my mother cleaning the kitchen. "Thanks for informing me that I'm not allowed to spend time with my aunt anymore," I said, not even trying to keep my attitude in check.

Don't even start with me, Violet," my mother said, staring at me icily.

I stared back with equal fury in my eyes. "Why is it such a big deal that I didn't say yes to Carter's invitation to prom?" I asked pointedly. This time I wasn't going to leave without an answer.

"I just think that you owe him a little more than that," she said.

"What could I possibly owe him?!" I asked, unsure of what she could possibly be talking about.

"You just stopped being friends for four years and you wouldn't even give him another chance!" she snapped.

"Excuse me?" I was livid. How could this woman who lived with me the entire time Carter and I weren't friends possibly think that it was my fault. "He stopped being friends with me," I reminded her. "I begged him to be my friend every day for two months. I gave up because he made it perfectly clear he didn't want to be friends with me. Now we are friends, which he probably doesn't even deserve, but I got over my petty grudge from four years ago and forgave him. So how about you forgive me for the things that are out of my control that you've been mad at me about for the last four years."

She stared at me in disbelief, as if I had just committed some sort of crime. (Well, if this house were a country, talking to my mother that way would be a crime.) "You know how important the Greenspan family is to this family," she said angrily, her voice shaking.

"Yeah, but I'm sure Carter hasn't been yelled at about this over at the Greenspan house!" I pointed out.

My mother narrowed her eyes at me. "Violet Irma Montgomery," was all that she managed to say.

I turned around and stomped up the stairs before giving her another chance to say anything.

I threw my backpack on the floor in my bedroom and wondered why the Greenspan family sat on a higher pedestal than my mother's own child. But then again, I had never really been that important to her.

I fed Pudge and sat down on my bed. I didn't really know what to make of this situation. Usually my mother just left me alone, so I couldn't figure out for the life of me why she was suddenly imposing herself in my personal life and getting mad at me for not making the decisions that she wanted me to make.

I pulled out my phone and sent the same message to both Carter and Willow. "My mom is being weird again." It said.

Willow replied saying "What now?"

"She yelled at me for not being friends with Carter for the past four years, as if it was my fault," I told her.

Before Willow responded there was a knock on my bedroom door. I didn't respond to it because I didn't really feel like speaking to my mother right now. I heard the doorknob turn and the door open.

"Vi," Carter said, standing in my doorway.

I bent my head back and looked at him upside down. "Hello," I said, not even mustering a surprised tone in my voice, though I was, probably foolishly, somewhat surprised that he was here. "I bet my mother was ecstatic to send you up here," I said in monotone.

"She seemed pleasantly surprised to see me," he said with a nod.

I sat up and turned to face him, pulling my legs up to my chest. "What's up?" I asked.

"You texted me and said that your mom was being weird," he pointed out.

"That I did," I agreed, wondering why he had taken that as an invitation into my house.

"So I thought if I came over, maybe I could observe her with you and we could draw our own conclusions," he said, almost as a question, moving across the room and sitting down with me on the bed.

"Sure," I said with a shrug.

"Well, Miss Montgomery," Carter said in his best 1930s private investigator impression. "Could ya tell me about the events leading up to the text message in question?"

I chuckled before diving into the story of that afternoon's events. "My mother said that I shouldn't have said no to going to prom with you, because I 'owe you' for not being friends with you for the last four years."

Carter stared at me in shock. "You owe me?" he asked, disbelievingly.

"Apparently it was my fault we weren't friends," I told him. "Apparently I was just trying to sabotage my family because I knew how important your family was to them."

Carter let out a peel of laughter. "Does she not know what happened?" he asked.

"I guess not," I told him. "But even if she did, she'd still find some way to blame me."

"How could she possibly blame you?" he asked.

"Well if it came down to it and I told her what really happened, her response would be something along the lines of 'Maybe you shouldn't have been so obsessed with him.'" I laughed.

Carter smiled, but didn't laugh with me, which didn't really bother me. I was used to thinking that I was funnier than I actually was.

"I'm sorry, Vi," he said after a few seconds of silence.

"It's not your fault," I told him.

"Well, it kind of is," he pointed out. "I'm the one who was stupid enough to stop being friends with you. It's not my fault your mom thinks it's your fault, but it's my fault it happened."

"Remember that time I told you to stop apologizing?" I asked jokingly.

"Yeah, sorry," he said with a chuckle.

We sat on my bed laughing for a few more minutes, and I almost felt as if we hadn't missed a day of being friends. After our laughing stopped, I got a more serious thought in my mind.

"I still don't know what she meant when she said she worked too hard for this," I said quietly.

"It was probably nothing," he said. "Don't think too much about it."

"But your mom said that things could be much worse," I reminded him. "It has to mean something.

He gave me a puzzled stare. "Should I ask my mom?" he asked me

"Yes," I told him. "I mean, it's our best chance at figuring out why everyone is being so weird."

"Okay, I'll ask my parents at dinner so I have a better chance at getting something out of one of them," he said. "I'll text you tonight and tell you how it goes."

With that, Carter got up and left my room.

I sat around my room for the next three hours waiting for a message from Carter. By seven-thirty there was no communication and I was getting antsy. I Picked up my phone and hit the new message button. I stared at the blank screen for a solid thirty seconds before throwing the phone back down on my bed.

At eight-twenty four I finally got a message from him. All it said was "No luck."

I groaned loudly and flung myself on my bed. After a couple of minutes of still and silence there was a knock on my door.

"Violet, you missed dinner," my mother said, opening my door.

"Sorry, Mom," I said, not moving my face out of my pillow. "I was… working on something."

"Oh, for school?" she asked.

"Not exactly."

"Well are you okay?" she asked.

"I'll be fine," I told her.

"Do you wanted to talk about it?" she asked, awkwardly stepping closer to my bed.

I lifted my head off of the pillow and stared at her. Honestly, she was the last person I wanted to talk to right now. I was super wigged out by the way she had been acting the past couple of days and was determined to find the cause of it

"I tried talking to you about it and you sent me to my room," I told her.

"Is it about Carter?" she asked.

"No," I said firmly. "It's about you."

She gave me a puzzled look as if she couldn't possibly know what I was talking about. "What do you mean?"

"Don't even give me that, Mom!" I said angrily.

"I honestly don't know what is going on with you, Violet. Why are you acting like this?"

"Acting like what, exactly? A teenage girl?" I asked. "A teenage girl who knows that everyone in her life is hiding something from her?"

"Did you ever stop to think that if *everyone* in your life is hiding something from you it's probably for the better?" she asked, not even trying to deny that something was being hidden from me.

"Did they ever stop to think that if it's something that affects me then maybe I should know about it?" I asked pointedly.

"Violet, you need to stop analyzing everything. Whatever you think is going on most likely isn't, and you have nothing to worry about," said my mother.

"I don't believe that for a second," I said, glaring at her.

"Why not?" she asked.

"If there was nothing going on, you, Trudi and Mrs. Greenspan wouldn't be acting like crack addicts trying to hide from Carter and me," I pointed out. "Unless *that* is what's going on," I said with a pensive look.

My mother looked appalled. "Violet Irma Montgomery!" she said with shock. "How dare you make accusations like that!"

"My GOD, Mother!" I said, which resulted in another shocked look at my use of God's name in vain. "You know what?" I continued. "This is why I didn't want to talk to you about this."

She continued staring at me as if waiting for me finish so I decided to use this opportunity to rant, which caused even more shock.

"I'll continue living the rest of my life in the dark, not knowing anything about myself or my life," I said dramatically.

"If it is something you need to know, Violet, you will find out in time," she snapped, opening the door and slamming it shut behind her after she walked out.

I sat on my bed thinking about the conversation we had just had. What did any of it mean? At times like this, I would usually go over to Trudi's and talk to her about it, but I knew whatever was going on, Trudi knew about it and wasn't going to give anything up.

I needed to talk to someone about this, so I just had one choice to make. Willow or Carter? After a few minutes of careful debate, I decided on Carter. After all, he lived just two houses down. Willow lived clear on the other side of town. She would understand.

"Meet me outside?" I texted Carter.

"Sure thing," came his response.

I put on a jacket and slipped out the back door without my parents noticing. I walked down the street, where Carter was waiting in front of Mrs. Downey's house, right between ours.

"What's up?" he asked, concern in his voice. It was slightly unnerving that I was asking him to meet me in the dark.

"Can we go to your yard?" I asked hopefully. His yard had always made me feel safe.

"Yeah, of course," he said.

We walked the hundred yards to his back yard in silence, but for some reason, his presence was oddly comforting. Once we were inside his fence, I sat down on the wooden swing between the ivy covered trees. Carter sat down on the ground in front of me.

"Is everything okay?" he asked once we were settled.

"For the most part," I responded.

Carter sighed. "Vi, what's going on?" he asked, staring at me knowingly.

"I tried to talk to my mom about what she had said yesterday and she got really mad at me," I started.

"Why? It's natural to be curious," he assured me.

"Well I might have accused her, Trudi and your mom of being crack addicts," I said with a solemn look.

He laughed. "Well that's bound to upset someone."

It's just been bothering me, you know?" I said. "Like, I don't know what she means when she says that she went through so much for me to not go to prom with you." I furrowed my brow. "And then she told me that if it was something that affected me I would find out 'in time'."

"Maybe it really isn't important," he conceded.

That wasn't good enough for me. "Carter, they're hiding something from me!" I told him, not trying to hide my frustration. "Whatever it is, it's something that affects me, and they're not telling me what it is! They're all just leaving me in the dark."

"They won't tell me either, Vi," Carter said.

"It doesn't directly affect you," I reminded him.

"How do you know?" He asked. "What if it's that we're actually twins who were separated at birth and one of us was adopted by the other parents?"

I stared at him for a second. "If we were twins, my mother wouldn't be upset about me not going to prom with you."

"Good point."

Then realization hit me. "But…" I started, not sure if I wanted to put the words in my head out in the open.

"But what?" he asked, apparently as concerned with the situation as I was.

"What if… I was adopted?" I asked. As soon as the words left my lips my heart dropped about a hundred feet. I buried my head in my hands. I shouldn't have said anything.

"Do you really think you were adopted?" Carter asked me, obviously not buying it.

"Well… I don't know," I said, sighing in defeat. "I mean, it's a stretch, but what else could it mean?" I asked.

"Any number of things," he said. "Or nothing at all."

He was probably right. I was sure I was over analyzing everything, just like my mother had accused me. But something just didn't feel right.

"You're probably right," I finally said, looking down at him sadly.

Carter reached a hand up and placed it softly on my knee. "We'll figure it out," he said in a soothing voice. "Or maybe we won't. But either way, I think you will be fine."

I gave him a weak half smile. "Thanks," I said quietly.

We sat there for what seemed like a really long time, but in reality was probably only five minutes. The whole time, Carter didn't take his hand off my knee.

I stood up off the swing, causing Carter's hand to drop. "Do you want me to walk you home?" he asked, standing up.

"That would be nice," I said quietly.

We walked across his yard in the dark. When we approached the gate, he held it open for me to walk through and closed it behind him. We walked down the street and up my driveway pausing at the back door.

Carter wrapped his arms around me in an awkward embrace. "It will be okay," he whispered into my hair.

I leaned into him, feeling way more comfortable than I probably should. "Thanks," I whispered back, barely audibly because my face was against his shoulder.

Carter let go of me and we stood face to face on the back step. "I missed you," he said after a prolonged moment of silence.

I stared up at him, unsure of how to react or where this was going. I nodded before telling him that I missed him too.

We stood on the back porch for a few more seconds just staring at each other. The way the moonlight reflected off of his green eyes and cast a shadow across his strong jaw made me wonder how I had resisted liking him over the past few weeks.

"I have to go," I said suddenly, turning away before this sexual tension built up any further.

"Goodnight," Carter said from behind me.

"Goodnight," I mumbled over my shoulder, pushing through the back door.

As I took the stairs up to my room I heard a creak on the landing. "Where were you?" my mother asked, furiously.

"I went outside to talk to Carter," I told her, annoyed that she was even asking after the speech she gave me tonight.

"Why didn't you tell anyone where you were going?"

"Oh," I said, raising my eyebrows, feigning mild surprise. "Is that what we do in this family? We tell each other things? Here I was thinking we did the opposite." I pushed through my bedroom door and shut it behind me. The last thing I needed right now was a hypocritical lecture from my mother.

Once inside my room, I got ready for bed. I sat down on the bed and took out my phone. I needed to text Willow to tell her about what had just happened. When I looked at my phone there was a message from Carter.

"I'm glad you chose me to talk to about this," was all it said.

"Yeah, me too," I responded, not even sure of what else I could say.

I pushed the new message button and typed "Wow, just had the weirdest moment with Carter. Meet me early tomorrow for details."

Trudi should have been a psychologist. At least then she'd know what she was talking about.

The next morning I was at school early just as I told Willow I would be. I sat alone for about ten minutes before she finally showed up. I knew I had to be careful what I said because if anyone heard this conversation and told Anna it could be disastrous. I also didn't want Carter to hear what I had to say.

"What happened?" she asked as she sat down.

I leaned across the table and started at the beginning. "My mom came in and yelled at me last night for the whole Carter thing again, and said it was my fault that we stopped being friends. Then basically admitted that everyone was hiding something from me but that it's better that I don't know."

Willow stared at me. "Okay, but where does Carter come in?"

"Let me finish," I said. "So I couldn't decide if I should call you and have you come over to talk about it or just go to Carter's and talk to him. So I decided on Carter because he was closer and it wouldn't be inconvenient for everyone," I looked at her out of the corner of my eye to see if she was angry with me. She didn't appear to be so I continued. "We were in his backyard, I was on a swing and he was on the ground in front me. He put his hand on my knee and left it there basically the entire time."

"That's all?" she asked.

"No, let me finish," I said impatiently. "After we were finished he walked me home," I leaned toward Willow and whispered the next part. "And he gave me this really long awkward hug and told me everything would be fine. Then when he broke the hug he told me that he missed me. I'm pretty sure that if I didn't turn around and go inside right then he would have kissed me."

Willow stared at me. "Do you really think he would have kissed you?" she asked.

"I don't know," I said. "Probably not, actually."

Just as we finished our conversation, Carter and Liam came to the table and sat down, Carter's seat inexplicably close to mine.

"Good morning," Carter said.

"Morning," Willow and I said in unison.

The rest of the day went by. As I walked to the parking lot right after school I saw Carter getting ready for baseball practice. "What are you doing tonight?" he asked me.

I stared at him blankly for a minute. Usually on Fridays I had dinner at Trudi's house, but I wasn't sure if I was allowed to go there anymore. I decided to go with it anyway, not wanting to repeat the incidents of the night before.

"Dinner with Trudi," I told him.

"Oh, okay then," He said, obviously discouraged.

I got into my car and then got back out and stood up. "What are you doing next weekend?" I asked him, just to see what he would say, knowing prom was next weekend.

"I don't know for sure," he said with a shrug. "The girl I asked to prom rejected me, so I don't know if I can risk showing my face."

"Wow, she sounds terrible," I said, trying to make him realize that I wasn't the idealized version of myself he had made up in his head when he refused to have anything to do with me.

"Everyone thinks so," he said. "Because of some rumor that someone even more terrible started. But she's not bad once you get to know her."

I snorted. "You must not know her very well."

"I'm trying to," he said. "And I don't give up easily."

I smiled at him and slid back into my driver's seat. I put my car in gear, pulled out of the parking lot and drove on autopilot to my aunt's house. I got out of the car and pushed through the door.

It was apparent that Trudi had just gotten home from work because she was still wearing her apron.

"Hey you," she said when I walked in.

"Am I allowed to be here?" I asked, somewhat angrily.

She rolled her eyes. "Of course you are. It's Friday!"

Fridays had always been the day that my aunt and I spent together ever since I was a little kid. But in light of recent events and my mother basically blacklisting us from each other, I wasn't sure that it was going to be okay for me to be here.

"Okay," was all I said.

"I rented movies!" she said, seeming much more giddy than usual.

"What's going on?" I asked with an eyebrow raised.

"What do you mean?" she asked

"You're acting like a child in a candy store," I pointed out.

"I'm just happy that you're here," she said with a cheesy smile.

I gave her a weird look and walked to the pantry. I pulled out a bag of popcorn and stuck it in the microwave for us to eat while we watched the movie.

"How have things been going?" she asked nonchalantly.

"Fine," I said with a shrug.

"What's going on with you and Carter?" she asked.

"Absolutely nothing," I said, avoiding her gaze.

"Are you sure about that?" she asked.

"Positive."

"Violet, you're going to have to tell me sooner or later," she said.

"If there was anything to tell you, I would have by now," I reminded her.

"Well your mom said that you snuck out to see him last night," she informed me.

"Well my mother doesn't know what she's talking about," I said.

"So who did you sneak out to see?" she asked, curiosity apparent.

"I saw Carter," I admitted. "But I don't really think it's considered sneaking out when you walk right out the back door and then tell your parent where you were the second you get back."

She stared at me for a few seconds. "And what did you and Carter do?"

"We talked…"

"About what?" she pried.

"About why you, my mother and his mother have been acting fifty shades of neurotic lately," I told her.

She stared at me again. "Really?"

"Really."

"Then why was it a big deal?" she asked.

This time I stared at her. "You're the one who's making it a big deal," I pointed out.

"Whatever," she said, grabbing the popcorn that I had just dumped into a bowl. "Let's go watch this movie."

We sat down in the living room and Trudi put the DVD in. "You could have invited Carter," she said.

"Why would I do that?" I asked, feeling anger well in me. I don't know why my aunt insisted that something had to happen between me and Carter. She was almost as bad as my mother at this point.

"Because you've loved him forever," was her simple response.

"Will you give it up, woman?" I asked, throwing a piece of popcorn at her.

"I just want what's best for you," she said with a smirk.

"I'm perfectly capable of deciding what's best for me," I told her. "Now shut up, the movie is starting."

We watched the movie in near silence. It was a gripping tale of childhood sweethearts growing up and going through the trials of life together before eventually getting married at the end of the movie. It was obvious that my aunt chose this movie on purpose to mess with my brain.

"Why did you do that?" I asked, when the credits began to roll.

"Do what?" she asked, not doing a very good job of looking oblivious.

"You purposely chose a movie that mocked my situation with Carter," I said, though as I said it, I realized that it wasn't exactly true. "Or rather, modeled the way you want the situation to be," I corrected myself.

"I have no idea what you're talking about," Trudi quipped, turning her nose up in the air. Sometimes my aunt's attitude was worse than mine.

I glared at her for a few seconds before she admitted her intentions. "I was just thinking that it could give you some ideas on how to get things started."

"I don't think you're getting that *I don't want to get anything started*," I reminded her.

She gave me a look that told me that she didn't believe a word I was saying. "Okay, Violet," she said in order to quell the argument before it got too out of hand. "Whatever you say." I could tell she didn't believe me, nor did she want to.

"I don't understand why everyone wants me to be with Carter!" I said angrily. "Don't Carter and I have a say in the matter?"

"Of course you do," she said, looking at me like I was crazy. "But I know you, Vi, and I just want to make sure that you're not avoiding your feelings just to prove a point to everyone."

"I'm past proving points," I told her. "Points go unnoticed in this family. If it was to prove a point I would probably date him and then start having a lot of angst to scare everyone. But making points? There's no point."

"Oh," was all she could manage as a response. "So you don't actually want to date him?"

"No. I don't. And I doubt he wants to date me either," I said pointedly. "So I wish everyone would just drop it. Unfortunately this family doesn't believe in that either!"

"Okay, fine," she said. "I won't push it anymore."

"Thanks."

I went home that night and laid in bed thinking about what my aunt said. I could admit that I found Carter attractive, and at one point, yes, I had liked him. So it was possible that my subconscious was making me think that I didn't like him so I could prove a point without my conscious brain knowing it?

And what was the deal with my family? Why was my love life all of a sudden so concerning to them? How had my mother been through too much for me *not* to go to prom with Carter?

I came up with a plan. There was only one week until prom, so I had to act quickly. The next morning at Saturday breakfast was where it would take place. I had to make sure to execute it perfectly or else it wouldn't work. I wasn't positive that it would work anyway because my family could be so unpredictable.

Phase one: Flattery is the most sincere form of ass kissing.

I walked down the stairs dressed in an outfit that my mother had deemed "nice," loathing this phase in my operation. I sat down at the table and poured myself a glass of milk. Pancakes were on the menu for this morning.

"Good morning, Violet," my father said through his paper as I sat down, not even bothering to look at me.

"Good morning, Daddy," I said back. I hadn't called him that since Liana was born. The first phase in my plan was to put my parents in a good mood by being the daughter they had always hoped for. The estimated time to complete this phase was approximately two days, because I might need to go to church in order to win them over completely.

My mother brought the dish of pancakes she had just made to the table and looked me up and down, a nervous look on her face. She could tell I was up to something. Otherwise, would I be wearing a light blue skirt suit? Nope.

"What's going on, Violet?" she asked after taking in my appearance.

"Oh, nothing, Mom," I said, trying to remain casual. "I just thought maybe I would give a few of these outfits a try and see how I like them." I mustered the most sincere smile I could manage.

She raised an eyebrow, but then smiled with relief, seeming to buy my answer. I decided I would try working in the church angle sometime during breakfast as well.

"How has work been, Dad?" I asked, launching my father into an overly enthusiastic story about a child biting him and getting his glove stuck in the kid's braces. I definitely didn't find the story interesting, nor did I want to listen to it, but I did, and nodded along pretending to be completely enthralled by it.

"And the library, Mom?" I asked when he was finished, causing my mother to explain very technically how the new filing system at the library works, which I didn't care about either. "Oh, that sounds much nicer," I said when she was finished so she would think I cared about her explanation.

Soon, I found an opening to work in the church angle, when my mother began explaining the Sunday school bake sale she was organizing to earn money to take Liana and Daniel's Sunday school class on a field trip to see Bibles being printed.

"I haven't been to church in a while, have I?" I pointed out solemnly. "Maybe I should go this week, you know, to show Jesus that I haven't forgotten about him." I added the last part to make my parents think that I believed in Jesus at all, much less cared what he thought.

My mother looked at me in disbelief. "Really?" she asked, placing her right hand over her heart in shock.

"Yeah," I said, before stuffing a forkful of pancakes into my mouth to avoid answering any more questions for a few moments.

"That's great," she said. "Isn't that great, Richard?"

My father grunted in response, which for him could be an entire conversation. My mother beamed at me as if I was the queen of England and she was meeting me for the first time.

"I'm really happy you've decided to be part of the family again, Violet," my mother said, still smiling.

It was nice to know she didn't consider me part of the family.

"Oh, and after church, I was hoping we could go dress shopping," I told my mother.

"That sounds great, Violet. What do you need a dress for?" she asked, her great mood apparent.

"Well, I'm considering going to prom with Carter," I told her, causing her to drop her fork on the table.

"Really?" she asked, hardly able to contain any amount of enthusiasm she was feeling at the moment. "That's great! What made you change your mind?"

"Well, there is one condition," I decided it would be better to bring this point up now rather than later.

"What's the condition?" She asked.

"I get to ask you one question and you have to *promise* to answer it honestly *no matter what,"* I informed her of my stipulation.

"Okay, what's your question?" she asked nervously.

"I don't know yet. But I can ask whenever it comes to me," I told her.

My father eyed me suspiciously across the table. Did he know what the big secret was? I'm sure he did, whatever it was.

"Oh, okay. Sure, honey," she agreed hesitantly.

After breakfast I went to my room and texted Carter. "So we need to talk about this whole prom ordeal," I said.

"What about it? There isn't an ordeal anymore," was his response.

"Well are you still free that night?" I asked.

"Yeah. I got rejected, remember?"

It was obvious Carter was bitter, which might make this difficult. Good thing I had accounted for that, which brought me to phase two.

Phase 2: Convince the former but not so current love interest that he still wants to go to prom with me.

"I know I've told you this before and you didn't like the idea, but I promise, this time it will be worth it," I told him.

"How?" he asked.

"Well, I kind of told my mom that I would go to prom with you, if she would answer any question I asked her in the future"

"Oh, so now I'm just a bargaining chip in your little blackmailing scheme?" he asked.

"It sounds bad when you put it like that…"

"Make it sound good then," he demanded.

"I will go to prom with you, and do all the girly get ready stuff. I'll put on a dress, heels, makeup, what have you. I will let you treat me like you would treat any date. I'll put aside any previous feelings of resentment and act as if none of it had ever happened," I texted him.

"So it will be a real date? Anything goes?" he asked.

Oh lord. What had I gotten myself into? I trusted Carter, of course I did, but I just wasn't sure what he meant by that. I wasn't going to do anything I didn't want to do just because I had to use Carter to blackmail my parents.

"Within reason," I said.

"That works for me."

Relief washed over me. Now that I knew I wasn't going to be forced into some compromising situation, I felt like this plan could really work out.

"Do you need to know what color my dress is to match the corsage?" I asked, adding a little face with the tongue sticking out.

"That would be helpful, yes," he said.

"Okay, well I don't have a dress," I told him.

"That's a lot of help, Vi, thanks," he said, but I was pretty sure he was joking.

"I'm going to get one tomorrow after church. (Kill me now.)" I responded.

"Oh, you'll be at church? See you there," he said.

"See you," I responded throwing my phone on the bed. I couldn't believe the lengths I would go to, church, prom, to find out one measly bit of information. It better be good.

I went about the rest of my day as usual, the only difference being that I went out of my way to please my parents. I did my homework and fed Pudge. I cleaned my room and bathroom and then cleaned Liana's room for good measure.

I went to bed at ten o'clock that night so I would be able to get up in time for church. I knew it wasn't required so if I was tired in the morning, I could bag out, but I also knew that that wouldn't help me, so I went to bed early.

The next morning I got up and put on another one of the outfits my mother had picked for me and went downstairs. My mother was rushing around the house trying to get things ready for church.

"Violet, can you help Liana with her hair?" she asked, walking past me into the kitchen.

I found Liana sitting on the floor in the living room with three headbands and eight different hair clips. "Can you get them all in my hair?" she asked me hopefully.

I smiled and sat down next to her. "I don't think so," I said, picking up a yellow headband that would match her dress. "How about this one?" I asked, sliding it behind her ears and up on to her head.

"Thanks," she said, getting up and running away. My sister and I weren't as close as I had wished we were, but my aunt had assured me that she and my mother weren't close when they were younger either. That came with big age differences between siblings. It also didn't help that I had a great deal of resentment for Liana when she was born because I thought my parents were replacing me with her. They never really tried to prove me wrong on that one.

I wandered into the kitchen looking for something to eat. My mother refused to cook breakfast on Sundays for fear she might be late to church or get something on her nice clothes. Instead she ran around the house like a chicken with her head cut off, which just stressed everyone else out. I wasn't sure if she really was that frantic about something or actually trying to stress us out.

Finally, the rest of the family was ready to go and we left for church. The church was only two blocks from our house in our small residential neighborhood, so when the weather was nice, they walked. This particular morning the sun happened to be shining full blast, so we trekked to the church on foot.

As we walked past the Greenspans' house, we were joined by Carter and his family.

"Good morning," Carter said as his family dispersed throughout mine.

I groaned. "I'm real excited," I said sarcastically.

Carter smiled. "It was your idea," he said, nudging me with his elbow.

"Whatever they're hiding from me better be good," I told him. "Or else I'm going to regret going to prom with you."

Carter gave me a sad look which caused me to crack a wide grin. I had to admit that flirting with Carter was fun, but it was purely innocent. I was pretty sure there were no feelings between us at all.

We arrived at the church and walked in. The greeters, who today happened to be two older members of the church who had probably attended my baptism, looked shocked to see me at church. Almost as if they couldn't believe that I could step through the doors without spontaneously combusting.

I sat awkwardly next to Carter in the pew. I hadn't been to church in so long I was almost unsure of what to expect. I knew it wouldn't be any different than it had been four years ago, but for some reason I couldn't help but be a little bit nervous.

The sermon began and I pretended to pay attention, but it was really boring and all I could think about was how I had to find a dress for the prom that I didn't want to go to, all while implementing phase three of my plan.

The service ended and we all stood around the church while my mother "mingled" with all the people who were there. She did this every week because she thought it was important to know every detail of every member of the congregation's week-to-week life.

"Do you want me to go with you?" Carter asked hopefully.

"Dress shopping?" I asked, unsure if that's what he was actually talking about.

"Yeah."

I stared at him for a second. "You want to stand around with my mother while I try on dress after dress after dress until I find one that I like and my mother approves of?"

"Sure," he said.

"I don't think you know what you're getting yourself into," I told him. "Besides, I think she's less likely to divulge family secrets with a third party in the car."

"You're probably right," he admitted. "Just tell me what color you end up with."

"I will," I said, smiling up at him. Something was fluttering inside my stomach, which was a feeling I hadn't felt since... Since Carter came into my tent while we were camping, come to think of it.

I dropped my head immediately and looked at my feet. I couldn't believe I was suddenly feeling like this around Carter. I couldn't believe he was changing my mind and proving me wrong.

"Are you okay?" he asked, reaching out and putting a hand on my arm.

"Yeah," I said, looking back up at him. "I just got dizzy. I didn't eat breakfast."

He nodded but gave me a sad look, almost as if he didn't really believe me. I couldn't say that I didn't deserve to be doubted by him. I had spent the last two weeks trying to avoid even being friends with him, much less going to prom with him or developing feelings for him.

After about twenty minutes of just standing around, my mother was finally ready to go. We departed the church and went back home to get the car. We drove silently to the mall, which was our plan A in the dress shopping dilemma. Since it was so close to prom, we weren't sure that we would be able to find a dress anywhere.

I needed to begin implementing phase three of my plan but I wasn't quite sure how to go about it. Every time I thought about bringing it up, I got queasy, so I decided to wait until I had found a dress, to make sure she was in a good mood.

If my life were a movie this would be a shopping montage set to a ridiculously upbeat pop song.

On the way to the mall, we stopped at Trudi's apartment complex.

"I told Trudi she could come," my mother said. "I hope that's okay."

"Sure," I said. If I told my mom that I didn't want Trudi to go, she would probably get really suspicious, since Trudi and I were so close. "I'll get her." I got out of the car and walked into the apartment, making my way back to her bedroom. "Trudi, we need to go," I called.

She walked out of the bathroom with her toothbrush in her mouth. She raised an eyebrow when she noticed my outfit. "Why are we in such a hurry?" she asked with a mouth full of toothpaste.

"I just want to get this over with," I whined.

She stopped brushing her teeth and stared at me. "Why are you resisting this?" she asked me.

"Honestly, Trudi. I don't want to go to prom with *anyone*. Not even Carter."

A devious look spread across Trudi's face. "We better get going," she said, pushing past me to walk through the bedroom door. I followed her out of the apartment and to my mother's car, where I got in the backseat so Trudi could get in the front seat.

The drive to the mall was about fifteen minutes from my aunt's apartment, and the entire way there they discussed what kind of dress I should get. They covered everything from length to color to neckline.

"I think we should go with a sweetheart neckline," my aunt stated. "Something red."

"She looks so good in peach though!" my mother argued.

"If we do peach, we're going to have to go with a halter," Trudi said.

"I don't want her in anything too low cut!"

I groaned in the backseat.

"What is it, Violet?" my mother asked.

"Do I get a say?" I asked.

"No," Trudi said. "You don't want to go, remember?" She turned back to my mother, "What about strapless? In pink?"

"That might be cute," my mother agreed. "And a corset back!"

Trudi squealed with delight, so I didn't have the heart to tell them that I would never wear a pink dress.

Finally, we pulled into the mall parking lot and got out of the car. We walked through the entrance of the mall, and I noticed that it was surprisingly slow for a Sunday afternoon. I was perfectly okay with this though, because I was already apprehensive about the rumors that would start when I showed up at prom with Carter. I was okay with spending one more week at school without abounding rumors of our relationship.

We went to Deb because it was the first store we passed that sold prom dresses. I found a rack full of dresses and started looking through them. I didn't even know what size I was, which might pose a slight problem.

My mother and Trudi had split up and were finding dresses that they liked, which were not only vastly different from each other, but were nothing I could picture myself wearing. The dresses chosen by my mother were modest, in various shades of peach, pink and light blue, while the dresses my aunt chose were, well, basically the opposite.

I tried on a couple from each just to make them happy, but I knew I wasn't going to pick any of them. After trying on six dresses and figuring out which size fit me the best, I asked if I could look for a little while. Both my mother and my aunt were reluctant to let me choose my own dress, because neither of them would like a dress that I picked out. It didn't seem to matter that I didn't like the dresses they were picking either. Truth be told, I didn't like dresses in general.

After five minutes of pushing dresses around on racks I found one that would be suitable. Neither my mother nor Trudi would like it, of course, so I decided to try it on without alerting them. If it fit I would tell them that I'm getting it no matter what before they could try to change my mind.

I slipped into the dressing room and locked the door. The dress was orange, floor length and strapless. The bodice was embroidered and sequined. It had an empire waist, and the skirt was several layers of tulle, which made it kind of poufy.

I stepped into the dress, pulled it up and zipped the back with no trouble. I wiggled around to make sure it wouldn't fall down. I picked my phone up off the bench and texted Carter.

"I think I found one," I said. I considered sending him a picture, but decided that he should have to wait until prom to see me in it.

I stepped out of the dressing room to find my mom and Trudi waiting outside.

"There you are," my mother said, preparing to hand me another pile of dresses.

"No, Mom," I said. "I found the one that I want," I said, gesturing to my dress.

My mother stared at me for a few seconds. "Are you sure that's the one you want?" she asked.

"Positive." I said.

"Don't you want to try on a few more?" Trudi asked.

"I've tried on twelve dresses," I told them. "I've liked one. This one. So if the two of you really want me to go to prom as much as you keep saying you do, you will be okay with me wearing this dress, okay?"

My mother and Trudi just looked at me. I realized that by having a bad attitude I was probably not going to be able to convince my mother to tell me her secret, but at this point I was willing to explore other options.

After a few seconds my mother nodded. "It's not so bad," she said.

"I actually kind of like it," Trudi agreed.

"Good, it's settled then," I said, turning and marching back into the dressing room. I took the dress off and hung it back on the hanger. My phone beeped and I saw that it was a message from Carter.

"What color?" it said.

"Orange," I responded.

"Really? Orange?" Carter replied.

"Yep. It was the only one I liked," I told him.

Once I had changed back into my hideous church outfit, we paid for the dress and walked back to the car. As we were crossing the parking lot, Leah walked past us, noticing that I was carrying a dress bag. Fortunately the dress bag was not transparent, so the dress couldn't be seen. She glared at me anyway. She probably glared at me simply because I am me, so I didn't worry about her assuming that I was going with Carter.

Persistence is part of his charm, but it's really freaking annoying.

When I got home, I took the dress up to my room and hung it in my closet. I texted Willow that I had gotten one and gushed to her about the details. I had to admit that having a dress that I actually liked made me *a little* excited for prom.

I changed into a pair of silky pajama pants and a baggy tie-dyed t-shirt, put on an upbeat Taylor Swift song and began dancing around my room, singing like an idiot. Nothing could damper this good mood. Or so I thought.

"We are never ever ever getting back together!" I belted out, just as someone knocked on my door. I practically jumped across my room and hit the pause button as fast as I could. "C-come in," I called through the door, settling myself in the desk chair, trying to make it look like I had been sitting there all along.

The doorknob turned and the door opened to reveal Carter standing in the frame. He had an amused expression on his face. "What was that?" he asked.

"What was what?" I asked, pretending I had no idea what he was talking about.

"What were you singing?" he asked.

"I wasn't singing anything?" I said, giving him a puzzled look.

He raised his eyebrow, but gave up. He sat down on the edge of my bed, facing me. "Where's the dress?" he asked.

"In my closet," I said. "But you can't see it."

"Why not?" he asked, standing up from the bed.

I jumped out of the chair and ran the few steps to the closet door. As soon as I got up, Carter tried to race me there. Luckily I was able to angle my body around his and press myself against the door so he couldn't open it.

Carter hit the door forcefully and fell down on top of me. I pushed him off and he rolled over so he was on his back on the floor in front of me.

"No fair," he said solemnly.

I cracked a smile. "You can see it on Saturday."

"I want to see it now," he said firmly.

"Well, that is just too bad."

We sat on my bedroom floor for about fifteen minutes without saying anything to each other. Carter got up and sat on the foot rail of my bed, looking down at me. "You're going to have to move eventually," he informed me

"No boys in my room after ten," I reminded him, pointing at the clock that said it was a quarter to five. "I think I can handle five hours."

Carter glared at me. "Your mom wouldn't kick me out," he said. "She likes me."

"Oh, you're so sure of yourself," I said. The truth was, my mother probably wouldn't kick him out, but I was going to let him sweat it out until 10 o'clock if that's what it took. It wasn't that important that he didn't see my dress before prom, but now that I had told him he couldn't see it, there was no way I was letting him.

I sat as close to the closet door as I possibly could so that he couldn't pull it forward. He remained perched on my bedrail, staring me down.

"Why can't I see the dress?" he persisted.

"Because it's supposed to be a surprise!" I whined.

"But you don't care about prom," he reminded me.

"Nope, not a bit," I lied. "But if I'm going to do it, I'm going to do it right."

"Did you get anything out of your mom?" he asked.

"No, she brought Trudi with us, so I didn't ask," I told him.

"So I could have come!" he said, pretending to be angry.

"Nope. I still would have said no," I told him, sticking my tongue out.

"You're killin' me smalls!" he said, dramatically falling backwards on to my bed.

I let out a small chuckle and remained firmly planted on the floor.

Carter sat up and gave me a disbelieving look. "You're not even going to check to make sure I'm okay?"

"You died," I reminded him, with a shrug. "There's not a lot I can do about that."

He narrowed his eyes at me. "If I was dead you would be upset," he said.

"I would?" I asked. "That's news to me."

"I see what you're trying to do, Violet Montgomery," he said. "And it's not going to work."

"Would you mind informing me of what I'm doing?" I asked. "Because I'm in the dark over here."

"You're trying to make me feel bad so I'll leave," he said.

"Oh yeah, that's definitely what I'm doing," I said sarcastically.

"Well I have to go anyway," he said, standing up.

"Okay. See you tomorrow," I said, looking up at him casually.

"Oh, I don't get a goodbye hug?" he asked, a crooked smile on his face.

I stared up at him. "I know what you're doing Carter Greenspan," I told him. "You want me to stand up so you can open my closet door and see my dress."

"No!" Carter said sarcastically. "Why would you accuse me of such a thing?" he asked, reaching down and grabbing my arm.

I tried shaking him off, but was unsuccessful. He pulled on my arm forcefully and dragged me across the carpet. My pants were slippery enough that they slid easily. As he reached for the doorknob I shouted "Wait!"

He paused and looked at me. "Yes?" he asked.

"If you see my dress before prom I'm not going to go!" I threatened.

"Oh, so you're going to tell your mother and Trudi that you're not going to prom after they took you dress shopping?" he asked.

"Yes," I said confidently.

Carter sighed and dropped his hand from the doorknob. "Fine," he conceded. I won't look at it. But it better be worth the wait."

I raised an eyebrow at him. "It will be," I promised.

He extended his hand toward me to help me up. I grabbed it as I began to pull myself up; Carter tried to pull me up, which caused me to slam hard into his chest, knocking the wind out of me.

"Ouch," I said breathlessly, taking a step back.

"I'm sorry," Carter muttered, looking away and rubbing the spot where I had hit his chest.

"It's okay," I said. Just then, I heard the doorknob turn and the door crack open.

"Vi," Trudi's voice came through the crack. "Dinner is almost ready."

"Okay," I said. I looked down and realized that my mother would not find this acceptable attire for dinner, even though no one would be here.

Trudi pushed the door open all the way. "Oh, hi Carter," she said, feigning ignorance. She knew he was here all along, but was pretending she had just noticed. "Would you like to stay for dinner?"

"Sure, Trudi," Carter said with a smirk. "That sounds great."

"Wonderful!" Trudi squealed. "I'll go set another place!" She walked off down the hall.

I glared at Carter for a second. "Why?" was all I could even articulate as a response.

He shrugged. "Why not?"

"My family is so embarrassing," I groaned, flopping down on my bed.

"It will be fine," he said. "Let's go."

"I have to change," I pointed out. "I'll meet you down there.

Carter left and shut my door behind him. I put on jeans and decided that if she asked I would just tell my mother that I didn't want to get one of my nice outfits dirty. I left the tie-dyed shirt on and walked down the stairs.

The conclusion? My mother is a drama queen.

When I walked into the dining room, everyone was laughing. "What's so funny?" I asked.

"Carter just told us how he fell on you trying to get to the dress," my mother said. "It was a hoot."

I rolled my eyes. My mother's vocabulary came straight out of an episode of Leave it to Beaver. I sat down at my usual spot, which in this case was between Trudi and Carter. Throughout dinner, my mother and Trudi talked to and joked with Carter. I remained silent unless spoken to directly. I was really annoyed that my family had invited Carter to Sunday dinner without asking me if I was okay with it first.

When dinner was over, Carter helped my mother and Trudi do the dishes, while I sat on the counter and watched.

"Violet, you could help, you know," my mother said.

"I could," I admitted. "But does it really take four people?"

"You're right," she said. "Stay put."

I stayed put gratefully. I knew that my mother could tell that I was annoyed, and I could tell that she was annoyed too, because no one had asked her if it was okay to invite Carter either.

When the dishes were done, Trudi announced that she had to leave. Soon after Trudi left, Carter said that he should probably go too.

"Thank you for dinner, Mrs. Montgomery," he said politely as he walked out the back door.

My mother sat down at the table and rested her forehead on her hand, letting out an exasperated sigh.

I sat down opposite her. "What's wrong?" I asked.

"Just stress, honey. You wouldn't understand."

I stared at her, astounded. "I wouldn't understand stress?" I asked, trying to keep my attitude level low. "I've been stressed for two weeks straight, ever since Carter started talking to me again."

"Really?" she asked, looking up at me. "Why was that causing you stress?" she asked, a confused look on her face.

"Mom, I hadn't talked to him in four whole years. And I had become okay with it, and then he all of a sudden decided he wanted to be friends again, and everyone expected me to just be okay with it, but I really wasn't."

"Is that all?" She asked, as if that wasn't a valid reason to be stressed.

"As a matter of fact, no, it's not," I told her bluntly. "I know that everyone is keeping a secret from me, and I would like to know what that secret is."

My mother sighed again. "Violet, now isn't a good time for this," she said, shaking her head.

"When will be a good time?" I asked. "Because I feel like whatever it is, it's something I should probably know."

"Will you just believe me when I say that whatever it is, you'll know it when you need to know it?"

"No."

"I'm serious, Violet. I don't want to discuss it."

"Well I do. Does that count for anything?" I nearly snapped.

My mother looked as though she was considering this. "Well I suppose I could tell you part of it," she said quietly. She sat up straight and looked at me. "You know that your father and I were relatively young when you were born."

"Yes," I said with a nod.

"Well, first of all, I want you to know that you were planned, and wanted. Nothing about your conception was an accident," she explained.

I stared at her, hoping this was as in depth she was planning on going into my conception. "Yes," I said, ushering her to continue.

"I was already pregnant with you, and Mrs. Greenspan confided in me that they were trying to have a baby as well."

I nodded again to show that I was keeping up.

"For weeks I would go to her house to support her while she took pregnancy test, after pregnancy test, but to no avail."

"Well it couldn't have taken that long," I said, trying to subtract Carter's date of birth from mine.

"It was only a couple of months," she agreed. "But after these first few weeks without luck, I sort of assumed that one of them was infertile. We were young. We didn't know that it could take a while."

I stared at her, not sure if I even wanted to know anymore.

"After a couple of months, she finally had a positive pregnancy test, and we were ecstatic," she said. "But, I still had doubts."

"What kind of doubts?" I asked, regretting it immediately.

"For a while, I thought that maybe, just maybe, Mrs. Greenspan had… tried alternative means of conceiving."

"Like what?" I asked. "Fertility treatments or something? What's so bad—"

"No," she cut me off. "She was only twenty-two. There would have been a lot of other options before fertility treatments."

"Then what?" I asked, curiosity outweighing my horror.

"Well, I assumed that the problem lied with Mr. Greenspan…" she trailed off.

"So you're saying… Mrs. Greenspan…"

"I thought so," my mother said. "And that's all you need to know."

"No," I said blatantly. "There's obviously more to it than that. Why else would it affect me? Or even you for that matter?"

I could see tears welling in my mother's eyes.

"No," was all I could say.

My mother nodded.

"Wait, so you're telling me…" my head was spinning. "Are you saying that…? Dad is… was… could be?"

"I thought so at the time," my mother said. "I just knew how quickly I had been able to get pregnant, and one thought led to another."

"What are you trying to tell me?" I asked. "Can you please just give me a straight answer instead of working your way around it?" I asked.

"At the time, when it took Mrs. Greenspan several weeks to conceive, I assumed that either she or Mr. Greenspan was unable to have children," she said.

"Yeah, I got that part," I said.

"So then when she was suddenly pregnant after weeks of negative pregnancy tests, naturally I assumed that maybe Mr. Greenspan wasn't the father."

"So you assumed that my dad was?" I asked, still not understanding.

"He was gone a lot," she said with a sniffle, a tear rolling down her cheek. "He was still in dental school, taking classes at weird hours. So naturally I was suspicious anyway. I knew how close they were, and how generous he was. I thought that maybe if she asked him enough, he would have given her the chance to have a baby too."

"That is the most ridiculous thing I have ever heard," I said. She shot me a glare, but I ignored her. "Did you discuss this with either of them?" I asked, pretty sure I knew the answer.

"Well no, not at first," my mother said, as expected. "I was happily married. She was happily married. I decided to just put it in the back of my mind. When Carter was born, he looked so much like Lisa; there was barely a trace of Mr. Greenspan, much less your father, so I didn't think about it again. Until you stopped being friends with Carter."

I gave her a puzzled look.

"It was obvious you liked him—"

"No, I didn't!" I interrupted.

"Anyway, I thought maybe Mrs. Greenspan assumed that you liked him, or that he liked you and told him, so that he wouldn't want to date you when you were older, and that's why he stopped talking to you."

I furrowed my brow. If that were the case, Carter surely would have brought it up, right?

"I tried to hint about it to your father, but he didn't understand what I was trying to say."

"Imagine that," I mumbled under my breath.

"When I asked Mrs. Greenspan why you and Carter weren't hanging out anymore, she just kept saying 'They're kids, they're not always going to do what we want them to,' but never really alluded to anything more.

"Finally, about four months after you stopped hanging out with Carter, your father and I were discussing whether or not we were going to force you to go to church. He was the one who fought for your side. He didn't think it was right to make you do anything you didn't want to do. I thought that we should make you continue to go to church. At some point in this argument I mentioned the whole situation. I told him you didn't want to go to church because Carter would be there. He said if you didn't want to be around Carter you shouldn't have to be. So that's when I asked him if he knew something that I didn't. He said he didn't know what I was talking about, and I assumed he was lying. But he kept insisting he didn't know what I was talking about. So I accused him."

"You accused him of knocking up Mrs. Greenspan?" I said, starting to get angry. My mother always assumed the worst in people, and now she was telling me that she had thought my father had cheated on her with Carter's mother? My head was still spinning. I didn't know what to make of any of this.

"Violet Irma," she said, before confirming it. "Yes, I had accused him of having an affair with Mrs. Greenspan. And he told me I was wrong for years. Then a few months ago, I brought it up to Mrs. Greenspan. She denied it as well, but for some reason I still didn't believe it. So, in order to prove it to me, I had her get a piece of Carter's DNA so we could run a paternity test."

"That wouldn't prove that they didn't have an affair. That would only prove that Carter wasn't his son," I pointed out.

"I know that, Violet," my mother snapped. "But I figured that if he wasn't Carter's father then it was less likely that he had had an affair—"

"Because you only wrongfully accused him of having an affair when Mrs. Greenspan got pregnant, instead of just being happy for her, and then when they both told you that they hadn't had an affair you couldn't have just believed them?"

"Violet Irma, do not speak to me that way!" she snapped.

I stared at her in disbelief for a few seconds before getting up and storming out the backdoor without another word. This entire scenario was ridiculous at best, and whether or not any of it was true, the fact that she would even think of it made me angrier than I even knew possible.

His best friend sounds like a delightful girl.

I could feel the hot tears making streams down my cheeks. I walked the few hundred feet to Carter's house and knocked on the door. Mrs. Greenspan opened the door. She had always been kind and welcoming to me, and now I felt bad about what my mother had just told me and I knew it was her fault. After all, it wasn't her fault that my mother can't just leave well enough alone.

"What's wrong, Violet?" She asked when she noticed I was crying.

"Nothing," I sniffed. "I need to talk to Carter though."

"Oh, come on in," she said, stepping aside to let me through the door. "He's in his room."

"Okay, thank you," I said. "I'm sorry for showing up here so late, Mrs. Greenspan," I added.

"Don't worry about it, sweetie," Mrs. Greenspan said, smiling as she walked to the stairs with me.

I walked up the stairs and made my way to Carter's room. I knew where it was from spending countless afternoons playing here when I was a kid. As I approached his door I tapped lightly on it to signal to him that I was standing outside his door.

After a few seconds, the door opened from inside and Carter was standing on the other side of the doorway. "Hey, Vi," he said. When he noticed the tears he automatically released his grip on the door knob and put his hand on my shoulder. "What's wrong?" he asked, genuine concern throughout his voice.

"I found out what the big secret was," I told him, wiping my face with the back of my hand. I wasn't even sure why I was so upset about this. I guess it was the idea that there was any question that Carter could have potentially been my brother even though I realized that there wasn't actually a question of whether or not Carter was my brother, and if he was I would have dealt with it. Maybe it was just that my mother had accused two of the most important people of my childhood with something so horrible. Maybe it was because she had tried to put it in my head that this was the reason Carter and I had stopped being friends.

"You're crying. I knew it! We're twins aren't we?" he said, attempting comic relief.

I gave him a half smile. "Not exactly."

"Do you want to come in? he said looking around his room to make sure it wasn't messy.

"Sure," I said, stepping through the doorway into his room. It wasn't much different than it had been the last time I was there; there were just a few more awards on the wall. I looked at the corkboard above his desk, which had been there for as long as I could remember. There was a picture pinned to it that I had colored for him in the second grade. I smiled, surprised he still had it.

It was a picture of a princess. I remember it distinctly. One afternoon while shopping with Mrs. Greenspan, she had said we could each pick out a coloring book. Following traditional child stereotypes, I chose a princess coloring book, while the one Carter chose was dinosaur themed. We got back to Carter's house and went to his room to color. Carter kept teasing me about how girly and lame my coloring book was, so I colored a princess and stuck it to his cork board. It had remained there ever since.

"That's kind of girly," I told him, pointing to it.

"Yeah, my best friend colored that for me," he said with a grin.

I sat down on the bed and pulled my legs up to my chest.

"Are you going to tell me what she told you?" he asked.

"Basically when your mom found out she was pregnant with you, the only logical explanation was that my father had had an affair with your mother and gotten her pregnant."

"What?" Carter asked, furrowing his brow.

"Well, they both denied it, and I believe them," I said. "And they already checked. You're not my brother. And my mother thought that the reason that you had stopped being friends with me was because you wanted me to be your girlfriend so your mother told you that you were my brother, and you stopped talking to me."

"That's ridiculous."

"Yeah."

Carter sat down at his desk, and we were silent for a minute. "She made your mom do a paternity test to prove it was safe for me to date you," I eventually said

"So I guess that ruins all of my chances of dating you," he said.

I bit my bottom lip. "I didn't say that," I said quietly.

He tilted his head and stared at me. "I know you though. And I know you would do anything to prove your parents wrong."

I shrugged. "I'm over them," I told him. I still wasn't sure if I wanted to date Carter, but I wasn't going to completely rule it out just to prove something to my parents.

"What do you mean?" he asked.

"I mean that I'm not going to stop myself from being happy just to prove a point."

He nodded to show that he understood, but didn't say anything.

"I just don't think it's fair for her to accuse them of that for no reason," I said. "I don't understand why your mom is still her friend."

Carter shrugged. "They've always been weird. Are you going to be okay?" he asked.

"Yeah, I guess. I just don't know if I'm going to be able to trust her, you know?"

"Yeah, I can imagine," he said. "You can stay here as long as you need to."

I looked over at the clock. It was eight forty-five.

"I don't have a ten o'clock rule," he said with a snicker.

I rolled my eyes. "Of course you don't," I told him. "Neither of your parents assumes adultery runs in your family."

"The only reason your parents have that rule is because they knew how awesome I was and realized that you would try to date me even if I was your brother, so they had to set boundaries."

"And that's why I'm not dating you," I said, throwing a pillow at him.

He caught the pillow and tossed it back to me, smiling the whole time. "I know. You don't date cocky assholes," he said. "You've said it a million times before."

"Oh, you're keeping count," I noted with a laugh.

"You know, I'm not always a cocky asshole," he said seriously.

"I know. Sometimes you're a persistent asshole," I told him.

He grinned cheekily at me. "Ain't that the truth?" he said, leaning back in his chair, stretching his back. As he stretched his shirt slid up, revealing his bellybutton. I looked away because at this point I didn't really want to be more attracted to him than I already was.

After a little bit of small talk, Carter moved over and sat on the bed with me. We talked until almost ten-thirty before I realized what time it was and decided I should go home.

"I'll walk you," Carter insisted. I was thankful for the offer because I hated being outside at night alone, even if it was only for a few seconds.

We quietly walked through his house, down the stairs and out the door. It was pretty chilly for a mid-April night and it showed when I let out a shiver. Carter sidestepped close to me, wrapped his arm around my shoulder and pulled me closer to him. I wondered if this is how he would have behaved if we had never stopped being friends. Would there be this level of attraction?

We approached my house and he gave me a squeeze with the arm that was already around me. "Goodnight," he said.

"Night," I reciprocated, moving away from him. "See you tomorrow," I said.

"See you," he said before turning and jogging back down the street to his house.

I went inside the house and walked quietly up the stairs to my room. I got into bed and replayed my evening at the Greenspan house in my mind. My feelings were a tangled mess of emotions and thoughts that I was having trouble processing. I was honestly attracted to Carter, but I still wasn't sure what I wanted.

It was apparent that he would be okay with dating, but he knew I wasn't, so he wasn't pushing it. That I was thankful for. He could be persistent, that was for damn sure, but he wasn't making me uncomfortable anymore. I liked the fact that he was okay with just being friends. It almost made him more attractive, which didn't help the confusion of it all.

I laid in bed for nearly an hour before my phone beeped. It was a text from Carter. Okay, maybe he was going to be persistent about this too. I opened the message. "I can't sleep ☹" it said.

"Me either," I replied. Immediately after I hit send, I realized that he might take that as an invitation to show up at my house in the middle of the night.

"This sucks. I would see if you wanted to come back, but we have school tomorrow, so maybe that's not a good idea.

"Yeah, I'll see you tomorrow," I replied.

I shoved my phone under my pillow and rolled over, drifting slowly into an uneasy sleep.

The rumor mill is churning. As per usual.

The next morning came much too early, and I grudgingly dragged myself out of bed to get ready for school. I put on jeans and a t-shirt, as usual. Since I already knew the 'big secret', and therefore didn't care about my mother's opinion anymore, I wasn't going to wear a hideous outfit just to appease her.

I came down the stairs into the kitchen, where my mother was giving the kids their breakfast. I made myself a bagel and ate it at the counter without saying a word to my mother.

"Good morning, Violet," she said after a little while.

"Yeah," I said, obviously not wanting to talk to her. I shoved the last bit of my bagel into my mouth, walked out the back door and went to school. I got there fifteen minutes before I usually do, but that was better than being at home and being forced to talk to my mother.

I sat down in the cafeteria and people watched until Liam, Willow and Carter showed up. While I was sitting there at my table, I heard some chatter behind me and decided to take a listen.

"She definitely had a dress bag," said a voice that I recognized as Leah's.

"Well did you see the dress? Maybe it was for something else," was said by Anna's whiney voice.

"The bag wasn't see through," said Leah. "But it looked like the bags from Deb. So it *had* to be a prom dress."

"No. There's no way," Anna said. "Carter wouldn't go to prom with her. He's not that stupid."

I rolled my eyes and continued listening.

"Well Liam and her weird friend are going together," Leah pointed out. "So maybe they're going together so they don't have to go stag or something."

Anna laughed out loud. "He wouldn't have to go stag. I told him just the other day that I will still go to prom with him. He's home free. If he's actually considering going to prom with that loser, it's because he lost a bet or he feels sorry for her or something."

"You're probably right," Leah said, though her tone was very unconvincing. "Why would he go to prom with the one girl he's known his entire life? The girl whom he stopped being friends with because you started a nasty rumor about her. The girl whose house he went to in the middle of the night to see if they could be friends again the day before you broke up."

"It's not like he's happy that we broke up!" Anna nearly shouted. "He's been begging me to take him back."

This time I actually laughed out loud. I heard Anna scoff because, at that point, she figured out that I had been listening. I turned toward her, smiled and gave a little finger wave. She narrowed her eyes at me and stomped out of the cafeteria, right past Carter who was walking toward me.

Carter came and sat down in the chair next to mine. "What was that all about?" he asked.

"Oh, the spawn of Satan was telling her little minion that you weren't stupid enough to go to prom with me, and that you've even been trying to get her back ever since she broke up with you. She heard me laugh about that, got mad and left."

"Interesting," he said, stroking his chin thoughtfully. "You know that's not true, right?"

"Duh."

"Okay, good," he said with a smile.

Willow and Liam arrived soon and we started going over plans for prom.

"Are you guys going to Steven's Friday night?" Liam asked Carter and me.

"What's going on at Steven's?" I asked, apparently out of the loop.

"He's having a pre-prom party," Carter explained. "Do you want to go?"

I shrugged. "I guess," I said. I might as well accompany my one night of teenage normalcy with another night of teenage normalcy.

"What about prom?" Willow asked.

"What about it?" I said.

"Where are you getting ready?"

"Your house," I informed her. "If I'm at home my mother and Trudi will be all up in my face trying to help and *no one* wants that."

"Is your dress really orange?" she asked.

"Yes," I said, looking at Carter out of the corner of my eye.

"What does it look like?" she asked.

'You can come over and see it after school," I said.

"I have to work," she reminded me.

"Wait a second," Carter interrupted. "Why can Willow see the dress but I can't?"

Liam let out a howl of laughter. "Dud, she wants to surprise you! How cute!" he said, causing me to blush.

"Whatever," Carter said. "Seriously though, Vi. Why can't I just see the dress?"

"Because I said you can't," I told him.

He glared at me for a second and then turned his attention back to Liam. "Did you pick up your tux yet?"

I turned back to Willow. "What about your dress?" I asked.

"It's green," Willow said with a shrug. "It was Charlotte's."

Charlotte was one of Willow's older sisters. She was four years older than us and looked almost identical to Willow, so the dress was bound to look great on her. It also worked out because Charlotte had graduated when we were in eighth grade, so no one at prom would even know that the dress had previously been worn.

When the bell rang we all went to our classes and the day went on as uneventfully as usual. I didn't even hear any rumors about whether or not I was going to prom with Carter. I attributed that to the fact that Anna didn't want to tell anyone that he was going to prom with anyone other than her.

I went to Trudi's immediately after school. I needed to vent about my mother. I didn't know if it was a good idea to vent to Trudi about her, but I didn't really know where else to go. Willow had to work and I was sure Carter was tired of hearing about it. Even if he wasn't, I didn't really want to spend too much time letting my attraction for him simmer. The more time I spent away from him, the better, and once prom was over that would be really easy.

I drove all the way to Trudi's house, so deeply immersed in thought that I almost didn't notice when my car started driving funny. I was about 100 yards from Trudi's parking lot, so I just pulled in and parked before getting out to inspect it. After I walked around my car about three times, I noticed that there was a very large nail sticking out of my front passenger side tire.

"Wonderful," I said out loud to myself.

"What?" I heard Trudi ask.

I looked up, and Trudi was leaning over the balcony railing. "There's a nail in my tire," I told her.

She stared at me as if she couldn't possibly know what I was talking about. "There's a *nail* in your *tire*?" she asked.

"No, I was making stuff up!" I said facetiously. "Yes, there's a nail in my tire. Will you call my dad, please?" I asked, bending down to examine the nail more closely. After a few minutes Trudi joined me.

"Wow, you really got it in there, didn't you?" she said.

"I was hoping to get it in a little farther," I said crankily. "What did he say?" I asked, referring to my father.

"He said he'll stop by when he gets off work, but he's not going to leave the office because you can't watch where you're driving," she relayed.

"I didn't think he would," I said with a sigh, standing back up. I turned and followed Trudi back into her apartment. Once inside, I flopped down on the couch. This was just my luck. This week was definitely not going my way.

"Well that sucks, Trudi said, sitting down next to me with two glasses of lemonade. I took one from her and sipped it.

"Yeah, just another blow to another horrible week," I sighed. "I never thought that prom would be the highlight."

"What do you mean?" she asked.

"I found out my mother's big secret last night," I told her.

"Oh," was all she said.

"I won't talk to you about it if it's going to make you feel awkward."

"You can say whatever you want. I'm indifferent."

"If you're indifferent then why wouldn't you just tell me when I asked?" I asked her.

"Because your mother didn't want you to know," she said. "If it was something she didn't care about you knowing, I would have told you no problem. But since she didn't want you to know, it wasn't my place to tell you, you know?"

"I wish she wouldn't have made such a big deal about it," I told her. "I'm mostly upset that everyone let me worry that something bad actually happened. I thought I was adopted for crap's sake!"

Trudi reeled for a second. "What exactly did she tell you?" she asked quietly.

"About how she accused Dad of having an affair with Mrs. Greenspan," I said, giving her a puzzled look. What else could I have been talking about?

"Oh, yeah, that," Trudi said distantly. "Well it must have been tough for her…"

"SHE DID IT TO HERSELF!" I shouted. "She couldn't leave well enough alone and threw around wild accusations. She made them get a paternity test. What if Dad had divorced her? What if she lost her best friend?"

"Well the important thing is that she didn't," she said.

I rolled my eyes. "She got lucky. I don't know how they put up with her anyway."

"Don't be ridiculous, Violet," Trudi said.

"That's probably why she's so distant. She probably thinks that it's my fault that she assumed that Dad boinked Mrs. Greenspan," I said angrily.

"How does that even begin to make sense?" Trudi asked.

"Well she was pregnant with me. So obviously it was my fault that Mrs. Greenspan wanted to get pregnant."

Trudi rolled her eyes.

"Whatever," I said turning away from her. I should have known better than to bring this up when I had no escape.

After about fifteen minutes of silence, Trudi spoke again. "What time should I come over on Saturday?"

"For what?" I asked. I knew what she was talking about, but I didn't want her to know that I was purposely avoiding it.

"To help you get ready for prom," she said.

"Oh," I said. "I actually promised Willow I would get ready with her at her house."

Trudi stared at me for a long second. "Are the Phans going to be okay with your mom and I being there?"

"Trudi, I don't need your help getting ready. It's just prom," I told her.

She stared at me again. "It's *just* prom?" she asked.

"Just prom," I repeated. "I probably won't even do my hair."

She glared at me for a second before turning the TV on. There was a rerun of How I Met Your Mother on, and she immediately became more interested in that than the conversation we'd been having, which was perfectly okay with me. After a couple of episodes, there was a knock on the door.

"How'd you do that?" my father asked gruffly as I opened the door.

"It was an accident," I said quietly, knowing he wasn't going to let up. "Can we just go?" I asked, looking over my shoulder to see that Trudi was still on the couch, ignoring us.

"We have to wait for the tow truck to get here and take your car in," he snapped.

Fortunately, it was only a couple of minutes before the tow truck showed up and loaded my car up. "We'll have to fix it in the morning," the tow truck driver told my dad, shaking his hand.

"Ask Carter if he'll take you over there before school," my father commanded.

"Okay," I said quietly.

We got home and my dad continued to gripe about how I destroyed my tire and should have been more careful with my driving. Arguing that I couldn't see the nail in the road didn't even faze him. It was all my fault.

I went to my room and shut myself in. I texted Carter to ask if he could take me to the repair shop in the morning.

"Of course," he said.

We worked out the details and I went to bed without eating dinner. I didn't want to face more scrutiny from my parents.

I've never been good at descriptive imagery, but luckily you probably don't want this visual.

Around two-thirty in the morning I woke up feeling nauseous. After about three minutes of queasiness, I got up and walked slowly to the bathroom. I turned on the light and waited for my eyes to adjust to the light before opening them and looking in the mirror. I looked positively ghastly. There were dark circles under my eyes and my skin was a shade of green that rivaled guacamole.

Upon seeing myself, I felt my stomach curl. I stepped over to the toilet and pushed the seat up in just enough time to hurl. I don't know how long I was throwing up, but my mother found me the next morning lying on the bathroom floor in front of the toilet. She flipped on the light and shrieked when she saw me. She probably couldn't tell if I had the flu or was passed out drunk.

"Violet?" she said uncertainly, as if she didn't know if it was actually me.

I groaned in response. My throat was dry, my mouth tasted like puke and my eyes were burning from the light.

"Are... are you okay?" she asked.

I groaned again, unsure of whether or not I was okay. There was a pounding in my head and my tongue was stuck to the roof of my mouth.

"You're covered in sweat," my mother pointed out. Thank you, Captain Obvious.

I slowly sat up and leaned against the wall. "I'm sick," I whined.

My mother opened the bathroom cupboard and pulled out a washcloth. She turned on the cold water and held the washcloth underneath it. After she decided it was cool enough, she rang it out and handed it to me to put on my forehead.

I couldn't help but think that if I were Daniel or Liana she would have put the washcloth on my forehead herself, but that's not how she was with me. I used the toilet to push myself up to my feet. I leaned against the wall, waiting for the dizziness to pass before I slowly walked back into my room and climbed into my bed. I looked at the clock and realized that it was only six in the morning.

My sleep was off and on for the next hour. My mother came into my room at 7:30 to get me up for school. I told her I wasn't going.

"You'll need to call Carter and tell him he doesn't need to pick you up this morning," she said. "Trudi and I will go get your car."

"Thanks," I muttered. I pulled my phone toward me and began to text Carter, but was interrupted by a coughing fit. I finally finished the message and rolled over to go back to sleep. After a few minutes, my phone beeped.

"Are you okay?" Carter had asked.

"Sick," I responded.

"Do you need anything?" he asked.

"I think I've got it under control," I told him.

It was sweet that he was offering to help me while I was sick and that just made me get more annoyed than I currently was. He was making it really hard for me to not like him.

"Okay. Get well soon!" he said.

"Thanks, I'll try."

I rolled back over and slept for a few more hours before waking up in a cold sweat. Around eleven I moved downstairs and took post on the couch, watching TV. After surfing the channels unenthusiastically I settled on the Ellen Show.

For the next four hours, I drifted in and out of sleep. The blankets were pushed down to the floor and pulled back up multiple times. The mountain of tissues three feet away was growing by the minute. My throat was dry and itchy, my eyes red and puffy. My nose was running like a stream. The Gatorade bottle on the coffee table was becoming less and less full. I had to pull my long hair into a bun on the top of my head because it was sticking to my sweaty back.

At a quarter to four, I heard the back door open and someone walk into the kitchen. I assumed it was my mother and paid no attention. I tried to fall back asleep through the clanking of dishes. I contemplated yelling at mother to be quiet so I could sleep, but didn't really have the energy.

About ten minutes later I heard footsteps coming into the living room. I shut my eyes to make her think that I was asleep. I really didn't want to talk to her right now. I heard a bowl being set on the table and felt a strong hand on my arm.

"Vi," Carter's voice whispered loudly, shaking my arm with his hand.

I blinked my eyes a few times pretending to wake up. "What?" I asked, confused.

"I brought you some soup," he said, gesturing toward the bowl on the table. "I hope you don't mind that I cooked it over here. I didn't want it to get cold."

"Thanks," I muttered, sitting up slightly.

"Are you okay?" he asked.

"I think so," I said, my voice hoarse from coughing.

Carter chuckled and sat down next to me on the couch. "You don't sound okay."

I groaned, but decided not to argue with him. "You're going to get sick if you stay here," I told him after a few minutes.

"You're probably right," he said, standing up. "Get some rest, I'll see you tomorrow."

"I don't know if I'll be well enough to go to school tomorrow," I reminded him.

"I didn't say I would see you at school," he pointed out.

I rolled my eyes. "Right," I said. "See you then."

Carter had barely made it out of the living room when the back door opened again.

"Hello, Carter," I heard my mother say as they passed in the kitchen.

"Hi, Mrs. Montgomery," Carter said. "I brought Vi some soup."

"That was very thoughtful of you, Carter, thank you," my mother said.

"No problem," said Carter as he pushed through the backdoor and left the house.

My mother bustled into the living room. "Eat your soup, Violet," she said. "Carter went through a lot of trouble to bring it to you."

"Yeah, I'm sure it was so much trouble," I said sarcastically.

"You think he just brought it over here for his health?" she asked.

"No," I said. "He risked his health to bring it to me."

"Exactly. Honestly, Violet, you should just give him the chance he deserves."

"Whatever," I said. I gathered up my blankets and pillow, grabbed my bottle of Gatorade and box of tissues and walked back up to my room slamming the door hard behind me. It was amazing how she could be so condescending even while I was sick.

The rest of the evening was spent in solitude. No one came upstairs to check on me. No one asked if I needed anything. No one even offered soup. I was okay with being left alone, it just amazed me how neglected I felt. Before I knew about my mother's evident resentment for me, I didn't really think much of it; but now I couldn't help but be reminded.

I fell asleep around eight that night. I had a strange dream about Willow and Carter turning into toes that I attributed to cold medicine.

I woke up the next morning feeling slightly better than the last. I got up and got ready for school like I normally did. I grabbed my backpack and walked down the stairs. Once in the kitchen, I popped a bagel in the toaster, and poured some Sunny D while waiting for the bagel to be done. Once the bagel popped up, I spread some cream cheese on it and walked to the door.

"Violet," my mother said as I approached the back door.

"What?" I asked, still not very happy with her.

"Your car is in the driveway," was all she said.

"Thanks," I said, opening the door and letting it close loudly behind me. It annoyed me that she had stopped me to tell me something that I would have figured out on my own in three seconds anyway.

I got in my car and drove to school. I sat in my spot in the cafeteria waiting for Willow. However, Carter was the first one to arrive.

"Good morning," he said.

"Morning," I said back.

"You look a lot better today," he observed.

"Thanks," I said, propping my head up on my hand. I was still really tired from being sick. "I feel a little bit better," I agreed.

"Did my soup help?" he asked.

I racked my brain, trying to remember if I had even touched his soup. I realized I hadn't so I improvised. "Oh yeah. It was great, thanks," I said, hoping that I was more convincing out loud than I sounded in my head.

"Anytime," he said with a grin. "Don't worry, I feel fine," he added.

I wasn't worried, but I wasn't going to tell him that. I had actually almost hoped he would get sick so I would have a reason to not go to prom. Okay, maybe I was a horrible person.

Willow and Liam showed up after a few minutes and neither of them could stop talking about how excited they were for prom. I was slightly annoyed because if you'd asked Willow a month ago she would have told you that she would never be caught dead at prom. Now it's all she could talk about.

I didn't want to say anything to her, but I think being with Liam had changed her. Part of it was probably because she hadn't even shown interest in Liam until the camping trip. Liam had liked her forever, and everyone had known. But whenever it was mentioned Willow shrugged it off like she didn't believe it and wouldn't have cared if she did. I was her best friend and I didn't even know that he had a chance with her. I wondered if it was possibly because she thought Carter was pursuing me that she gave in to Liam's chase.

"Vi, where do you want to go to dinner?" Liam asked, pulling me out of my trance.

"What? Oh, I don't care," I told them. Honestly, I hadn't even thought about it. I knew that traditionally groups went out to dinner before prom, but I hadn't really thought about the fact that they were going to do traditional prom stuff.

"How about Taquito's?" Carter suggested.

Willow groaned. "I want sushi," she said.

"Willow hates Mexican food," I pointed out.

"Well what about Flounder's then?" Carter asked.

Willow stared at him. "If I'm going to eat sushi, it's not going to be gross American sushi," she said pointedly.

"Well I'm not Japanese. I can't tell the difference," Carter said.

Now Willow was glaring at him. "I'm not Japanese either," she pointed out. "I'm Vietnamese."

Like most Asians, Willow tended to get offended when anyone called her the wrong nationality. Luckily for her the topic of ethnicity didn't come up often. Since I had known her only one person had said anything remotely racist to her face, telling her to "go back to her country". "I was born in Ohio!" she had shouted. After that, no one said anything about it.

"Sorry," Carter said quictly, his cheeks growing red.

"It's fine. Maybe we should skip the sushi though," Willow said. "You probably wouldn't be able to handle real sushi anyway."

Carter narrowed his eyes at her. "What's that supposed to mean?" he asked.

"Oh nothing," Willow said. "Let's go to Koibito's and find out."

"Fine," said Carter. "Koibito's it is."

"Are we getting a limo?" Liam asked.

"I think it's a little late for that," I told him.

"What do you mean?"

"Prom is in four days," I pointed out. "There is like one limo service in this town. They're probably all rented out."

"Good point," he said.

"Besides that, let's just save the limo for senior prom," I said.

Everyone at the table raised their eyebrow and it took me a while to figure out why. By the time I had realized what I said to shock them the bell had rang signaling that it was time for another day of humdrum classes.

By the time the day was over I was exhausted, physically and mentally, so I decided to go straight home and relax. I was still recovering from being sick. I went to my room as soon as I got home and put on a pair of ratty sweats and an oversized t-shirt, grabbed my laptop and climbed into bed.

Go big or go home, I guess.

The next three days went by more uneventfully than I even thought possible. The plans for prom were all set, there were no abounding rumors about whether or not I was going to prom with Carter, but plenty of rumors about how Anna had told Carter she would, under no circumstances, go to prom with him, and that if he had to settle for going to prom with me instead, so be it. He told her that going to prom with me wouldn't be settling, but would actually be a step up, which made her even angrier.

On Friday morning, my internal clock decided that it was time to wake up half an hour before my alarm went off. I laid in bed for fifteen minutes, wondering why my subconscious made me wake up so early. Then I realized that Steven Travis's party was tonight and that must be what I'm anxious about.

I reminded myself that I didn't have to be party ready for school and rolled over for another half an hour of sleep. When my alarm clock did go off I got up to get ready for school, trying not to overdo it in anticipation for the party that night.

School was uneventful, as usual, maybe even more so, aside from the pre-party chatter that was going around about what was going to happen at Steven's. It sounded like a lot of people were going to be there, which made me a little bit nervous. Not just because it was my first party, but also partly because I was going to show up with Carter and I knew the rumors would fly.

Carter, Willow, Liam and I decided that we would all ride together in my car.

"I'll be the designated driver," Liam offered.

"What?" I asked.

"What do you mean?" he said.

"Why do we need a designated driver?" I asked dumbly.

"Well you're not going to drive drunk are you?" he asked.

"Oh, duh," I said. It didn't even occur to me when they said we would be going to a party that there would be alcohol involved. The notion that there would be alcohol made me even more apprehensive about going. I had never been drunk and didn't know what to expect.

I went through the rest of the day unable to think about anything other than the party. Since I had never gone to parties before, no one assumed that I would be going and talked to me about it, which I was thankful for, but anytime I was near Carter or Liam in the halls, they were stopped and interrogated by random people.

By the time school was over, I was almost ready to throw up from nervousness. I was annoyed with myself for being this nervous about the idea of alcohol at a high school party.

The fact that I was this bothered by the whole alcohol thing really alarmed me as well. What kind of high school student feels like they are going to throw up all day just because they realize there would be alcohol at a party that they were going to? Most of them would be psyched. It wasn't like anyone was going to force alcohol down my throat. I could say no. I could tell Liam that I would be the designated driver. Actually, that's exactly what I would do.

After my last class, I set out to find Liam. I searched the hallways of the school for about five minutes. He and Willow usually stayed after school for a little while, so I didn't think it would be hard to find them. I was wrong. Finally, I saw Carter and decided to ask him for help.

"Have you seen Liam?" I asked.

"He already left," Carter told me. "What do you need him for?"

"I was just going to tell him that I would be the designated driver tonight so he wouldn't have to worry about it," I said.

Carter laughed. "Vi, did you think Liam was offering to be the designated driver to be nice?"

"Well yeah."

"No," Carter said with a chuckle. "Liam doesn't drink."

"Oh…" I said, feeling really dumb. "But I don't drink either."

"Yeah, only because you've never had a drink," he said.

Carter and I turned and started walking down the hallway to go to the parking lot. "Why doesn't Liam drink?" I asked.

"His dad, grandpa and uncle were all alcoholics," Carter said. "He didn't want to risk it."

"What do you mean 'were'?" I asked, genuinely curious.

"Well, his grandpa died of liver failure when Liam was a kid," he told me. "His uncle got into other drugs and is in jail, and his dad went through a twelve step program and got cleaned up. He's been sober for seven years now."

"Oh wow," I said. I had never even considered the possibility that someone I knew had a more dysfunctional family than me. "Good for him," I said finally. "And good for Liam for knowing that it could happen to him."

"Yeah," Carter said. "Liam is a surprisingly responsible guy."

"That's good," I said, suddenly thinking of Willow and feeling more at ease.

We got to the parking lot and had to part ways to go to our own cars. "See you tonight," Carter called as he walked away from me.

"Later!" I called back.

I got home about five minutes before my mother and the kids. I was sitting on the kitchen island eating an apple when they walked through the back door.

"Violet, get off the counter," my mother scolded as soon as she saw me. I slid down off the counter and stood leaning against it while I finished my apple.

"I need you to go to the grocery store with me after dinner tonight," my mother told me. "We're having a potluck after church on Sunday and we need to get the stuff to make the twice-baked potatoes. Since you're going to be busy tomorrow we'll have to get the ingredients tonight."

"No can do, Mom," I told her. "I have plans tonight."

My mother scoffed at me. "Doing what?" she asked.

"Hanging out with Carter," I said, hoping that would be enough for her to be okay with it.

"Oh, she said, pausing to look at me. She had the must dumbfounded expression on her face. "Well, have fun," she said with a sigh.

"Thanks," I said. With that I turned and walked out of the kitchen. I went upstairs to my room and tried to decide what to wear to the party.

I searched through my closet to find something to wear but was unsuccessful. I called Willow.

"Hello?" she answered.

"What are you wearing?" I asked in panic.

"Jeans and a t-shirt…" Willow said.

"To the party?" I asked, slightly perplexed.

"I don't know," she said. "What's it matter?"

"I don't know what to wear!" I nearly shouted into the phone.

I could almost hear Willow roll her eyes at me through the phone. And truth was, if it were anyone else I would be rolling my eyes too. I had never cared about my appearance, so I shouldn't be freaking out over what I was going to wear to a party that would inevitably be infested with people I didn't like anyway.

"Vi, calm down. I'll come over before we go get the guys and help you pick something out."

"Okay," I said calmly. "I'll see you later." I hung up and threw my phone on my bed. I started pulling out clothes that seemed like they might be appropriate party attire. I sorted through my jeans and found the pair that I thought looked best on me and set them aside so that I could tell Willow they were the ones I wanted to wear. I arranged the shirts by style and then rearranged them by color. Then I found a few skirts that I had, just in case.

At six twenty-four, Willow walked through my bedroom door wearing denim shorts and a flowing floral top. I was in the process of holding all the shirts up with possible camisoles to see how they looked.

"Whoa, did your closet throw up?" she asked, looking around my room.

"I still can't decide," I griped, tossing the pair I was holding down on the bed.

"You're putting too much thought into it," she said. "Just find something you like. Here," she handed me a teal Aèropostale t-shirt with the words "Here Comes the Sun" scripted across the front. "Wear this with those jeans," she said, pointing to my favorite jeans that I had flung across the head rail of my bed. She picked up a yellow camisole and tossed it to me.

I changed into the outfit that Willow had picked and moved to the vanity, where I wiped my face off with a make-up removing wipe. I played with my hair for a few minutes, trying multiple things before Willow got fed up and pushed me down into my desk chair.

After about twenty-five minutes of curling irons and hairspray she finally allowed me to stand up and look at myself. My hair was pulled into a curly side ponytail that cascaded over my left shoulder. I smiled at Willow in the mirror and began putting on my make-up. After a dab of concealer, a flurry of powder and the customary swipe of mascara, I was party ready.

Willow and I walked down the stairs. My intention was to sneak out the back door without my mother noticing us, especially because Willow wasn't always subtle in situations like these. My plan failed when we reached the bottom of the stairs to find my mother in the kitchen cooking dinner.

"You girls look nice," my mother noted. "What are you doing tonight?"

"Double date, Mrs. M!" Willow said as we walked past, "Gotta go, or we'll be late!"

"Have fun," she called after us as we walked out the door.

"What was that?" I asked Willow once we were safely inside my car.

"Well, it's kind of a double date," she pointed out.

"Yes, it might be, but I don't want my mother to think that I'm dating Carter!"

"Let her be happy for a while," she teased.

"We're getting our hopes up," I said with a chuckle.

I started my car and pulled out of the driveway. I slowly drove the couple hundred feet to Carter's house and stopped. I honked the horn to tell Carter and Liam that we were there and after a few seconds they emerged from the house and got into the car.

Carter, sitting in the backseat, directed me to Steven's house because I had never been there before.

"We're here," Carter said as we pulled up to a large mansion right by the river.

"This is his house?" I asked, slightly dumbfounded. "It's huge!"

'You didn't know that Steven Travis had a big house?" Liam asked, as if it was completely obvious.

I knew his step dad was some sort of movie producer, but I didn't think he had been on any movies big enough to pay for a house this big. "I guess I just didn't think about it," I said. This house was ridiculous. It was two stories with an attic over part of it. There was a full balcony across the entire front side of the second floor. The wrap-around porch had large white columns. It was painted light blue with dark blue shutters and roof.

I parked the car and we got out. Liam automatically attached himself to Willow once they were within two feet of each other. Carter came and stood near me as I was just standing there, still in awe of this house.

"We can go inside, you know," Carter said.

"I-I-I know," I said nervously, not sure if I wanted to go in. We moved up the porch and toward the door, greeting various people that we passed. Carter was very popular, especially among the ladies.

We stopped for a minute by the door to talk to Tyler and Erin, both already had a drink in their hand. After a few minutes of small talk, Carter directed me through the door.

Once inside the front door I was even more amazed by the inside of the house. It was immaculate. "Are you sure having a party here is a good idea?" I whispered to Carter.

Carter chuckled. "He has parties here all the time."

"Does stuff get... broken?" I asked, feeling really naïve for even asking.

Carter smiled. "Sometimes. Usually people are careful," he told me. "He doesn't invite dipshits who are going to screw everything up for him."

"Do... do his parents... know?" I asked quietly.

Carter chuckled again. "Yeah. They kind of let him get away with it. They feel bad for being so busy."

"Oh..." I said. Again, sometimes I forgot to remember that some families might be more dysfunctional than mine.

We took a walk around the house so I cold marvel in how nice it was. Finally, we ended up in the kitchen. It was a kitchen my mother would kill for, and let me remind you, my family wasn't exactly short of money.

"Do you want something to drink?" Carter asked.

My heart did a backflip. I was still super apprehensive about the whole idea of drinking. What happened if I drank too much? I didn't know what I was like when I was drunk and I didn't want to embarrass myself. But I was curious. Maybe it wouldn't be so bad if I was careful about it. I just needed to make sure I didn't drink too much.

"Sure," I said quietly.

"What do you want?" he asked.

I stared at him for a few seconds. "I don't know," I told him, not wanting to have to point out again that I had never drank before.

"Right," he said, opening the fridge. "How about a Mike's Hard Lemonade?" he asked.

"Sure," I said.

"Strawberry, cranberry, lime or original?" he asked.

"Cranberry," I said, prompting him to pull a bottle of dark reddish liquid out of the fridge and pull the lid off. Next, he pulled a Corona out of the bottom drawer and opened it for himself.

I took a tentative sip of my cranberry lemonade and decided that it wasn't that bad. After finishing nearly half the bottle, I was starting to feel the proverbial buzz that everyone talks about, which when it's happening, literally makes you feel like you're buzzing. *That's probably why they call it that,* I noted to myself mentally.

I followed Carter around like a lost puppy for the next half hour, but he made continuous conversations, so I didn't feel as weird about it. Eventually, when I was about two-thirds of the way through my second bottle, we sat down on a little dock that stuck out into the river. We were silent for a few minutes before Carter sighed and set his bottle of beer, which was still half full, to the side.

"What's wrong?" I asked, trying to hold my composure.

"Nothing," he said, though he was very unconvincing.

"Tell me," I urged.

"I just probably shouldn't really drink," he said.

"Why not?"

"Well…" he started but stopped.

"What?" I persisted.

"It doesn't matter," he said.

"Just tell me."

"If I drink too much, I might try to kiss you," he blurted.

The words danced around in my head. "Do you want to kiss me?" I asked, not able to look at him. I could feel my cheeks getting warm, but I didn't know if it was from the alcohol or because I was embarrassed.

"Well yeah," he said, his voice barely audible.

"Are you drunk?" I asked.

"No."

"Well then why don't you just kiss me?" I asked.

"Because I know it's not what you want."

"It's been a while since you asked me what I want."

"Well, I guess so," he said. "But you were so hesitant to even be friends with me that I couldn't imagine that you would want to kiss me."

"Did you consider that maybe I was scared it would just happen all over again?"

He paused for a second. "What does that say about me?" he asked quietly.

"That you're kind of a jack ass," I said.

He sighed. "Yeah, I guess I am."

"You still haven't asked me what I wanted," I pointed out.

"What do you want, Vi?" he asked.

"I want you to kiss me," I said. Call it liquid courage, but that was what I needed to make a solid decision about Carter. I could definitely feel the alcohol, but as far as I could tell it wasn't hindering my judgment *that* much.

He looked really taken aback, but after taking a few seconds to compose himself, he leaned in and pressed his lips gently to mine. He broke the kiss, but lingered on my face for a few more seconds before moving back.

He leaned back, holding himself up with his arms. I bit my lower lip and looked away. I probably wasn't any good at kissing (since I wasn't very experienced with it), but I didn't want to let on to that, so I stayed silent. I didn't want to make things more awkward than they already were.

After a minute or two of silence, Willow and Liam came and found us.

"What are you guys doing?" Willow asked, obviously more intoxicated than not. I was actually kind of worried she was going to fall off the dock.

"Nothing," Carter responded, almost too quickly.

I looked away from my friends again, embarrassment washing through me. I took another swig from my bottle to see if it would make me feel any better. It didn't.

"Bro," Liam said. That was all he said, so I was sure they were engaging in some sort of silent communication. That became more apparent when Willow sat down next to me, on the opposite side as Carter.

"What's up," she asked quietly.

"Well…" I said, not sure I wanted to talk about it. Not here anyway, where they could all see me. I felt that if I said anything I might burst into tears. Was alcohol a depressant?

"Well?" she asked.

"I'll tell you later," I whispered.

"Come on, Willow," Liam said. "Let's go check out the balcony!"

Willow got up and slid her arm around Liam's and they ran off.

"They're cute," Carter said as they walked away.

I sighed. I couldn't help but want what they had. It had happened so fast, but they were so happy together. "Yeah," was the only response I could articulate.

"I've always kind of wondered…" Carter said quietly. "Do you think that could have been us?"

The question confused me. "You mean if we hadn't met until recently?" I asked.

"No, I mean if I wasn't dumb enough to stop being friends with you. Do you think we would have ended up in a cute relationship?"

I wanted to tell him that it wasn't too late for that to happen, but refrained. "Maybe," was all I said. I wondered if I was so bad at kissing that weeks of pursuing me was ruined with just one kiss. Then I remembered the first time we ever kissed. Had he been able to tell that I was a bad kisser, even then? We were only nine years old.

I pulled my knees up to my chest and held them tight. I didn't want him to notice how upset I was, but I needed the comfort right now.

"Are you okay?" he asked.

"I guess," I said.

"What do you mean?" he asked.

"I mean, it's nothing I shouldn't have expected," I told him.

"You're being vague," he pointed out. He didn't really sound annoyed, more concerned.

"Am I a bad kisser?" I asked bluntly.

He gave me a puzzled look. "Of course not," he said. He sounded sincere, so I didn't really worry that he was just trying to spare my feelings.

"Then why don't you want to kiss me again?" I asked pitifully.

"I didn't say I don't want to kiss you again, Vi," he said with a chuckle.

"Then why haven't you?" I asked.

"Because you're drunk," he told me. "I'll kiss you again tomorrow, okay?"

"Okay," I agreed.

We got up and walked around the party some more, mingling with the people we knew. After a while, my plan to be careful kind of went out the window and I ended up consuming a few more beverages than I had originally planned. The rest of the night was a blurry blur.

I couldn't remember if I was going to prom or a WWE event.

Saturday morning, I woke up in my own bed, wearing sweatpants and the camisole from the night before. I was really confused about how I got there and how my clothes had been changed. I could barely remember the night before. I found my phone on the table by my bed so I could text Willow.

The moment I opened my eyes it felt as though someone had hit me on the head with a sledgehammer. My mouth was dry and I kind of wanted to die. I looked at my phone and there was a message from Carter. "Aspirin and orange juice will help," it said. Oh my. Was Carter the one who put me to bed and changed my clothes for me? If so, it was a thoughtful gesture, I guess, but I would have been fine in my jeans. I didn't need him getting fresh with me if I was already passed out.

"What exactly happened last night?" I texted him back.

"I didn't pay enough attention to make sure you weren't drinking too much. You threw up in a bush and cried the whole way home, saying Jesus was going to be really mad at all of us. We got you into your room and Willow changed your clothes. Do you feel okay?"

"I feel like death," I replied.

Just as I as formulating what I was going to tell my parents, there was a tiny knock on the door. "Violet, are you awake?" my mother said quietly through the closed door.

"Yes," I groaned.

She opened the door and poked her head in. "How are you feeling?" she asked.

"What?" I asked. Did she know? I was panicking internally, but couldn't give it away in case she didn't know.

"Carter and Willow said you had food poisoning from the restaurant you ate at last night," she said. "It was nice of them to bring you home like that."

"Oh yeah," I said. "I'm feeling okay."

"Are you still going to go to prom?" she asked.

"Probably," I said. "Will you bring me some orange juice?"

'Sure," she said, shutting the door behind her. I got up slowly and was much less dizzy than I thought I would be. I found some aspirin and set it next to my bed before climbing back in.

My mother opened the door and brought my orange juice to me. I thanked her and she left quickly. I used the orange juice to chase the aspirin and sat in my bed until it worked. While I was waiting I got texts from both Willow and Liam making sure I was okay. I told them both that I was fine, because I thought my headache might be subsiding.

A majority of the day was spent sitting in bed trying to wait out my hang over. Around two o'clock, I decided I should probably get out of bed and go over to Willow's to get ready for prom. Our dinner reservations weren't until six, but I wanted to make sure that I was ready. And beside Willow's house, we had at least two other houses we had to stop at so our parents could dote and take pictures of us. I pulled a t-shirt over my camisole and stayed in the sweatpants.

I put on a pair of black flip-flops, which I realized I would have to wear to prom because I neglected to get real shoes to wear. I stuffed some makeup and various hair products into a bag and pulled the dress out of my closet.

Once I got downstairs, I told my mother that I was leaving and would see her around five. My house was the first stop on our list because I was sure that my mother would be the most obnoxious and want to take the most pictures.

I got in my car and drove to Willow's house, barely paying attention to what I was doing. I got out of my car and let myself into the house. Willow's parents didn't believe in doorbells.

"Hello Mr. Phan," I said when I saw him. "Mrs. Phan," I called toward the kitchen, where I was sure she was. She always made pho whenever Willow had anyone over. I went up the stairs, into Willow's room and threw my stuff on the bed.

"Well hello, Sister Christian," Willow said as I walked into her room.

I gave her a confused look, and she told me the same thing Carter had said about how I kept telling everyone Jesus would be mad at us.

"Right," I said. "Well he would be."

Willow snickered at me before picking up my dress and unzipping the bag so she could see it. "Nice," she expressed when she saw it.

We spent the next couple of hours doing our hair, asking each other for opinions and redoing it. Willow opted for curls pulled over her right shoulder, secured with a rather large, rhinestone barrette. I braided the front of my hair back into a messy side bun. Once we were both satisfied with our hair styles, we moved on to makeup. The best part about getting ready at Willow's house was that she had her own bathroom with a giant mirror and a rather long counter. We could spread all of our stuff out on the counter and there was room to spare.

We finished our hair and make-up around four forty-five, which left us about five minutes to get into our dresses before the guys got here. Willow pulled on her dress and I zipped it up for her. She did the same for me once I had my dress on. She put her shoes on, while I slipped my feet into my flip flops and luckily we were down stairs before the guys showed up. I didn't want to do the clichéd first-sight-on-the-staircase thing that they did in all the movies.

When Carter and Liam finally got there I couldn't believe how good Carter looked in his tux. Suddenly I had a flashback to the night before. Had he really kissed me or had I hallucinated it? Did people hallucinate when they were drunk? I didn't really know.

Carter smiled when he saw me and the butterflies in my stomach flapped their wings harder than ever before. He held out the corsage he had gotten for me, which matched my dress surprisingly well. I held out my hand and he slipped it onto my wrist.

Since we were already there, Mr. and Mrs. Phan took their pictures first. They only took about ten minutes because they knew that our time wasn't expendable. I hoped that my mother would realize the same thing.

We went to my house next and luckily my mother only took half an hour to take pictures and exclaim repeatedly how good everyone looked. Even more luckily, Mr. and Mrs. Greenspan and Trudi were all at my house taking pictures at the same time. After a quick stop at Liam's house, we were able to make the restaurant on time, where Tyler and Erin were waiting for us.

Up to that point the night had been going much better than I had thought it would. We had a good time at dinner, talking and laughing. No one spilled anything, which was also a plus. We got to the dance in time for Willow, Erin and I to criticize the other girls' dresses while Carter, Liam, and Tyler stood around awkwardly.

When the first slow song came on, Liam came and swept Willow away. Carter walked slowly toward me, took my hand and pulled me into him to dance. After maybe thirty seconds of dancing, there was a tap on my shoulder.

"Excuse me," said a shrill voice over the music that I immediately recognized as Anna's.

I turned around to see what she wanted. "What?" I asked.

"You're dancing with my boyfriend," she said angrily. "I don't really appreciate that."

By this point I was really fed up with Anna. Carter might not have been my boyfriend, but he certainly wasn't hers either. "Newsflash," I said, using my best attitude voice. "*You* broke up with him. Forgive me for thinking that made him fair game."

Anna scoffed at me. "You know what, Violet?" she said my name as if it tasted disgusting in her mouth. "I didn't work my ass off in middle school to pry the two of you apart so that he could go to prom with you instead of me!"

I stared at her for a second.

"Go away, Anna," Carter said from behind me. "You're interrupting my dance with my *date*." He put particular emphasis on the word date, hoping Anna would get the picture and leave us alone.

Anna glared at us for a second before stomping away toward Leah, who was sitting alone at a table.

Carter turned me around and resumed dancing position.

"She can't take a hint, can she?" I asked, annoyance present in my voice.

"Apparently not," he said, pulling me closer to him. The song ended and we were rejoined by Liam and Willow.

"What was that about?" Willow asked me, nodding in Anna's direction.

"Apparently her and Carter are still an item," I said sarcastically. "She was offended that I was dancing with her boyfriend."

Willow laughed.

The DJ played some fast songs, and a couple more slow songs, all of which I danced with Carter, while Anna sat in the corner glaring us down. Carter was a surprisingly good dancer, and even more to my surprise, I wasn't bad either.

About halfway through the dance, when we were all sweaty and out of breath, I told Carter I would go get us some punch. I was walking toward the refreshment table when Willow intercepted me. "Come to the bathroom with me," she said, grabbing my wrist and pulling me toward the bathrooms. Once inside, Willow began adjusting her dress and fixing her makeup.

I was staring at myself awkwardly in the mirror waiting for Willow to finish when the door opened. Anna came in, followed by Leah. Anna shot us each a glare before wedging herself in between Willow and I, bumping us both with her hips in the process.

Willow scoffed. "Excuse *me,*" she said, an extra hint of sass in her voice.

"You're excused," Anna said in mock politeness.

I glared at her through the mirror, trying to gather the courage to finally say what needed to be said. Eventually, I had it. "I don't know what your problem is, Anna," I started. "But you broke up with Carter. He is free to dance with whoever he wants. He's free to date whoever he wants, for that matter. I don't know why you're having trouble understanding that. Maybe all the bleach seeped through your skull and made your brain stop working!" Even after the words had left my mouth I still couldn't believe that I had said it.

Before I knew what was happening there was a stinging handprint burning my right cheek. The next thing I knew I was on the ground pulling her hair and throwing punches. Willow and Leah were trying to pull us apart. When they finally got me off her, Anna and Leah ran out of the bathroom leaving me and Willow in there alone.

Willow didn't seem very happy with me, and her words exemplified that. "What did you do that for?" she asked, glaring at me.

"She hit me first!" I shouted. "Did you expect me to just take that?"

"You're allowed to have the initial reaction of wanting to punch her in the face," Willow agreed, quoting Trudi. "But that doesn't mean you have to act on it!"

"Sorry," I muttered.

"I'll go get the guys. You probably shouldn't stay here like that," she said.

I stood up and looked in the mirror. My hair was messier than it had been to begin with. My lip was bleeding and I had a sizable bruise forming under my left eye. After a couple of minutes, Willow opened the door again.

"Let's go," she said. I followed her out of the bathroom and to my car. Everyone was silent as I drove to Willow's house, where I dropped both her and Liam off.

"I'm sorry," I told them again as they got out of the car.

"Yeah," was all Willow said.

Liam reached through the open driver's side window and put his hand on my shoulder. "Remind me to stay on your good side," he joked.

As I pulled away from the curb Carter looked over at me. "That was… intense," he said.

"You probably weren't expecting two girls to throw punches over you at prom," I pointed out.

"I definitely wasn't," he admitted. "Though, I can't say that I'm impressed."

"I wouldn't be either," I said. "I'm not very impressed with myself."

"You embarrassed me, Vi," he said. "Willow too."

"I'm not proud of it, okay?" I said. I could feel tears burning my eyes, and I willed them not to fall out. "I don't know why I did it." I pulled up next to the curb at Carter's house.

"I don't know why you did it either," he said angrily, getting out of my car and slamming the door. The resulting tears that began to flow down my face stung as they hit the broken skin.

Well that worked out then.

The next day I sat on Trudi's kitchen counter holding an icepack on my throbbing black eye.

"I can't believe you hit her!" Trudi exclaimed.

"I'm not proud of it, okay," I said to her. I had to repeat those words so many times; from when I said it to Carter last night, when I had to tell my mother this morning, and now with Trudi.

"You should be!" She said. "It's not every day you get to fight the bitch that screwed up your life."

"Well everyone is mad at me because of it," I told her. "I ruined everyone's prom."

"Since when do you care about prom?" she asked.

"I thought I didn't," I explained. "But then I was there, and it was a lot more fun than I had expected."

"Well they won't hate you forever," she said, trying and failing at being encouraging.

"Carter went four years without talking to me. I think he'd be fine without me."

"Well it's a good thing you don't like him then," she said knowingly.

"Actually..." I bit my lip, which I had forgotten was hurt, and winced.

"What? Don't tell me you've changed your mind!"

"Well..." I wasn't sure where to start. "He kissed me on Friday," I said, looking away.

"What?" she asked, raising an eyebrow.

"We were at a party," I started.

"Were you drinking?" she interrupted.

"Yeah, but anyway, we were sitting on this dock..."

"Were you drunk?" she asked.

"I was, a little bit. He wasn't," I said.

"Well what happened?" she asked impatiently.

"If you'd just shut up, I would tell you!" I snapped. "He told me that he couldn't drink because if he got drunk he would kiss me. I asked if he wanted to kiss me and he said yes, but he wasn't going to because it wasn't what I wanted. So I pointed out that he had never asked me what I wanted. He asked me what I wanted, I told him I wanted him to kiss me, and he did."

"Was it good?" she asked.

"As far as I could tell," I told her. "But it was just one kiss and he didn't try to kiss me again after that. So I got upset and asked if I was bad at it and he said that I wasn't but he wasn't going to kiss me again because I was drunk and that he would kiss me tomorrow."

"Oh," Trudi said.

"Well tomorrow was yesterday and he didn't kiss me again. But that's probably a good thing," I said, using my tongue to feel the scab on my lower lip.

"So do you like him?" she asked.

I stared at her for a second before saying "Uh, yeah. Did you not get that out of this explanation?"

She stared at me for a few seconds, picking at the sandwich that was sitting in front of her. After a couple of minutes of silence there was a light knock on the door. "I'll get it," Trudi said getting up. I remained on the counter, not wanting to see whoever it was at the door.

I heard the door open and some hushed whispering. Trudi reemerged into the kitchen. "There's someone here who wants to see you," she said, stepping to the side and revealing Carter.

"Hey," he said quietly.

I removed the icepack from my face and set it down next to me on the counter. "Hello," I said. I was glad that he wanted to talk to me enough that he tracked me down, but I half wished that he would have waited to track me down until half my face wasn't swollen.

"I'm sorry I yelled at you last night," he said. "You didn't deserve it. I know you wouldn't get into a fight without a good reason."

"She hit me first," I pointed out.

Carter chuckled. "Jeff texted me and said that she was at his church this morning and has two black eyes."

I gave him a little half smile. "I still shouldn't have done it."

Carter shrugged. "Maybe."

I looked down sadly, unable to think of anything to say.

"Vi," Carter said, prompting me to look at him. He moved closer to me and placed his hand under my chin, turning my head so he could look at my black eye.

"That's a nice shiner you got," he said with a smile.

I didn't want him looking at me at all, much less examining my facial bruising. Unexpectedly, he leaned in closer and lightly kissed my mostly undamaged upper lip. He pulled away and looked at me. I was slightly taken aback but tried to let it show.

"Vi, will you just be my girlfriend already?" he asked.

"Oh, you would date a girl who looks like an MMA fighter?" I asked teasingly.

"That's kind of my type," he told me with a smile. He took my hand and pulled me off of the counter, through my aunt's apartment and out the front door.

"Where are we going?" I asked.

"I don't know," he said as we walked down the sidewalk.

We tried to walk into the sunset, but it burnt us, so we went elsewhere.